JOHN NEWTON CHANCE

◆

# THE DEATH WATCH LADIES

*Complete and Unabridged*

# LINFORD
*Leicester*

First published in Great Britain in 1980 by
Robert Hale Limited
London

First Linford Edition
published 1998
by arrangement with
Robert Hale Limited
London

British Library CIP Data

Chance, John Newton, 1911 – 1983
The death watch ladies.—Large print ed.—
Linford mystery library
1. Detective and mystery stories
2. Large type books
I. Title
823.9′14 [F]

ISBN 0-7089-5342-5

Published by
F. A. Thorpe (Publishing) Ltd.
Anstey, Leicestershire

Set by Words & Graphics Ltd.
Anstey, Leicestershire
Printed and bound in Great Britain by
T. J. International Ltd., Padstow, Cornwall

This book is printed on acid-free paper

# THE DEATH WATCH LADIES

The detective had only to find an uncle who had gone missing, and whose hat had been found. But when he arrived at the house of the van Deken family, his ideas of an easy job vanished. He was beset by each member of the family taking him aside to tell a different story of what had happened, and which incriminated another member of the family. Before long the detective didn't know quite who was dead, missing, or about to be dead!

*Books by John Newton Chance*
*in the Linford Mystery Library:*

# SCREAMING FOG

# 1

Marley was dead. Dead as Mutton. And as unfashionable. I always regret the passing of Mutton, the grand roast saddle with its crisp, light fat; the boiled leg on its bed of good winter vegetables, and the sharp caper sauce. They kill sheep too soon these days. In pursuit of fatless, tasteless, chewing gum lean.

Anyhow, Marley was dead and so I came to Linfield at midday on December 6th. It was a quiet little town, living in the past except for its apparent ignorance of parking laws.

A room had been booked for me at an inn called The Keys, which was just along the street from the gates of the house where my business was to be.

It was one-thirty when I got there, and there was nobody in the bar but the landlord, a shortish, baldish man, polishing a glass behind the counter.

He looked at me as if wondering what

on earth I was doing there and went on polishing his glass. I told him why I had come.

'Oh,' he said, polishing. He held up the glass and looked at it against the light. 'Yes.' He put the glass down. 'Mr. Gaunt.'

'Yes,' I said, for that was the name I had decided to use.

'Missus hasn't quite finished the room,' he said as a thunderous row broke out overhead. 'That's her now, vacuuming.

'Daughter will get you some lunch. Fresh fish, come ashore ten o'clock this morning. Fetch it myself. Got no time for frozen muck. I always say the purpose of a freezer is preserving corpses for the Post Mortem.'

I warmed to the innkeeper and said I would have a sole grilled on the bone. He went out the back. I heard him talking to a woman. I looked along his shelves and picked out the labels of white Worthington.

When I ordered one he regarded me with a faint warmth in his dark eyes and carried out the pouring ceremony.

'Catch me own salmon out in the Estuary,' he said. 'Take it down to Totnes meself for smoking. That way you know what it is. I use the imported variety to sole me boots. It keeps the dogs to heel.'

He never smiled, it seemed to me.

I began to lead him on about the town and its trade and people. He said a lot, all as severely critical of people as he had been of frozen food.

And then he said, 'And of course, Cock of the Walk, though she's a woman, Mrs. Van Deken. Her husband made millions from cocoa beans and they came and bought the town, almost, and the gates along here lead to the house. One of her sons booked your room.'

'I know. Ralph,' I said, 'but didn't know his mother was alive.'

'Perhaps she isn't. She lives like God, ordering this, that, them and those regardless. Hardly ever see her. She sends the others running for her. Three daughters, two sons. All devoted to her money. Two married, but had to give up and go back to Mama. Makes you angry to watch it going on.'

'You know Ralph?' I said.

'I know three of 'em,' he said. 'Sometimes they sneak in the back door for smoked salmon and a decent meal. Mama don't allow no eating out.'

He cocked his head and looked at me.

'You going up there?' he said.

'Yes, so I'm told.'

'Better not let on you're staying here. She'll have you out and up there, pigging it with the others on oatmeal and dried figs.'

'Are they vegetarians?' I said, anxiously.

'On and off,' he said 'What Mama does they all do. One time she got mad on eating grass. All sorts of grass. All different kinds of grass. Grass boiled with treacle, steamed grass with walnuts, walnuts with fried grass pancakes. Just like cowpats, but with less flavour, as the tramp said.'

He turned away.

'No, you want to watch out for her. Don't get drawn in. You can't even pay to get out from there.'

The daughter, he called her Annie, came in and laid me a table over by the fireplace. She was a fine big girl, blonde and brown skinned. She smiled and showed a dimple in her cheek.

'Sit you down,' she said, holding her empty tray against her big bosom like a shield. 'I'll bring the fish.'

I saw the innkeeper watch her go out, then look towards me as if to see if I liked other things beside food.

If Mama Van Deken tried to grab me away from this pub I was going to be very cross indeed.

\* \* \*

Ralph came in by the back door about ten past two. He spoke with the innkeeper as he came into the bar, then he came across to me.

The introductions over, he sat down facing me across the table.

'I thought you'd be older,' he said.

The landlord came out from behind the bar and went round, locking the doors. Then he went back behind the bar and disappeared in the direction of the kitchen.

'You know what I wanted you for?' Ralph said, watching me.

'You said your uncle was missing. That was all.'

'God! that fish! It's torment,' he said, staring at my plate.

'Sorry. You can have the skeleton. There's nothing else.'

He chewed a thumbnail and watched me as if not sure how to go on.

'He's dead,' he said, uncovering his face. 'I think he's still in the house.'

I looked at him. He seemed worried, even fearful of something.

'How long has he been missing?'

'Ten days. He turned up suddenly, you see. Clarence Marley was father's stepbrother. Black sheep type. Been away for years. Suddenly turned up. Mama turned on The Black. We were tensed up for two days, wondering what she would do.

'Then suddenly, Clarence wasn't around any more. We all wondered where'd he'd gone. He'd seemed so determined to

6

stay. Then suddenly — presto! nothing to be seen.'

'You can't be suspecting your mother.'

'Of course not.'

'You asked each other what could have happened?'

'Of course.'

'Three sisters? One brother?'

'Yes. The Feeble Five.' He grinned at last. 'We do it for the money.'

'You asked Mama where he'd gone?'

He stopped grinning.

'Nobody asks Mama. If Mama wants to say, Mama says.'

'Did she seem to notice he'd gone?'

'As if he'd never been there.'

'And still nobody asked her?'

He leant across the table.

'Nobody asks Mama because it's no bloody good asking Mama. Ask her a question and she goes on about something else as if she's got a rota of rehearsed speeches about Something Else for the Occasion, and goes on and on.

'By the time she stops, you've forgotten.'

'I see. But why do you think Clarence didn't go?'

'Nobody saw him go, but Gertrude found his hat. The hat he came in.'

'Where?'

'It had been in the river but the stream washed it ashore. The river goes through our ground.'

'That's a tributary which goes into the estuary direct?'

'No, it swings west a bit, then hooks on to the bigger river from the south and about a mile on they go into the Estuary.'

'By now Clarence could have been washed out to sea.'

'No. We found a net across. Poachers. Downstream from where we found the hat. Trying to snitch our salmon. They had to run and left the net. It wasn't spotted at once.'

'Your grounds large?'

'Fairly. We have — or Mama has — a couple of registered layabouts who call themselves horticultural operatives.'

'So you and your brother and sisters believe he is dead?'

'Yes.'

'Why not call the police?'

'Police and Mama would not mix. To tell the truth. I don't think they'd win the contest.'

'Am I likely to succeed?'

'Now I've seen you, yes. Handsome, mature, strong, ladies' man, clearly. Yes. Mama has a weak spot though we never get near it.'

'Flattering nonsense. You are kidding yourself. Have you really become so hopeless?'

'You are not kind.'

'As I recall, you asked me here to be unkind.'

'Oh no.' He cheered up. 'No one can be unkind to Mama.'

'Very well. Now let's start again — from my side.

'Why do you want to find out what happened to Clarence?'

'To clear our minds.'

'Well, supposing by some long shot, I clear your minds, and it shows Mama killed him. Then what do you do?'

'The quorum would then decide.'

'The five children?'

'Of course.'

'Are there grandchildren?'

'Oh no. My sister and I would never have risked it. Mama would have taken such offspring for herself. She is very much like that. The family is hers.'

'I heard you had left your wife.'

'Divorced. Yes.'

'Was that anything to do with Mama?'

'In a way — yes.'

'In what way?'

'My wife said I would have to decide whether to marry her or my mother.'

'I see. And it was one of your sisters who married?'

'Yes. Laura.'

'What happened to her marriage?'

'Laura found she didn't like her husband.'

'I'm not sure I understand what you mean.'

'I see what you're getting at. Mama kept suggesting he wasn't good enough and in the end Laura agreed. She wanted a child, but, as I said, was frightened Mama would take it over and she wouldn't be able to stop her.'

'Do you think that was possible?'

'It was impossible she wouldn't. I told you, the family is hers.'

I sat back.

'What happened to your father?'

'Mama ate him. She consumed him. He became a limb of hers, and that was the end of him.'

'He died a long time ago?'

He thought a moment.

'Oh — twenty years. Maybe one or two more. We were all away at school. Committed suicide, you know.'

'No. I didn't know. How?'

'Threw himself off the tower balcony. There's a tower at the house, you know. We called it the Cocoa Finger.'

'The inquest verdict?'

'Misadventure. Said he fell off. Kindest.'

'Is the memory of your father's death persuading you to imagine his brother died violently?'

'Oh, I see what you mean. No.'

'Clarence knew your mother before he went away?'

'Oh yes. We saw him often when we were small.'

11

'Your mother didn't object to him, then.'

'Oh no. She likes men.'

'But you say she didn't like it when he came back?'

'I don't know what that was about,' he said. 'But you must remember he was away a long time.'

'I see. Now, so far, Mr. Van Deken — '

'Call me Ralph, otherwise you'll get so confused later on.'

'Right. So far you have given me a picture of your mother as a dictator, a matriarch, a warder, an operational egoist and oppressor, who would think nothing of murdering her brother-in-law.'

'Well?' he said, as if asking whether there could be something unusual about that.

★ ★ ★

'Well, what is it you're asking me to do? Find that she murdered Clarence?'

'No. Find Clarence, what's left of him.'

'But if we find Clarence's dead body,

12

it can't stop there.'

'Let's find it first.'

'Right.' The daughter came in and removed my things on her tray, smiled and went out. Ralph patted her bottom when she turned to go.

'Anything else you want to know?'

'Quite a lot. You have three sisters and a brother. Do they live in the house?'

'Of course. Where else would be so comfortable and cheap?'

'What do they do?'

'Piddle around. They're waiting. We're all waiting to roll in the cocoa.'

'Do you mean you all do nothing at all?'

'Oh, some paint, write poems, novels. Collect things. Make things. Distill poisons.'

'What are poisons for?'

'Oh pests. That sort of thing. Dudley's trying to sharpen knives so he can split hairs. Haute science, as it were.

'Of course, you'll think we're potty — did I mention a fee? A thousand a week. We'll all chip in, you see. Oh, and I forgot Fanny.'

'Fanny is what. A dog? A horse?'

'Oh no, Mama's companion, house-keeper, confidante, lover — who can tell to what red hell the conspiring soul may lead?'

'It would help if you expanded.'

'Well, she's a tall woman, big-built, sometimes forbidding and sometimes one must fight to keep the door of one's bedroom shut.'

'She is your mother's confidant, you say. So she might know things you wouldn't?'

'She would, not might. Sometimes Mama likes to be put upon, I suppose as a relief from her continual battering of our heads. Fanny obliges. It's very odd to see if you come across it suddenly. Fanny telling Mama what to do and sit down and beg forgiveness and so forth. Either it's said or makes you gawp.'

'Fanny has been there a long time?'

'Fanny came as a girl to do Mama's hair. Mama is very proud of her hair. Comes down past the bum. Magnificent. And Fanny came to groom it. And then Father threw himself off the tower and Fanny was Mama's All, you might say.'

'But what about her daughters?'

'Mama doesn't like her daughters. To Mama, they are rivals.'

'She likes her sons?'

'It is difficult for us to avoid being crushed to those overblown breasts in the ecstasy of possession. I have often nearly suffocated.'

'And she was possessive towards your father?'

'We always think of Father as a poor old male spider. Do you know about spiders? No? Well, the male walks for bloody miles through the undergrowth to find a mate, and when he finds her he gets so overdone with copulation he dies from exhaustion. She does not, as is generally supposed, eat him alive but slays him with possessive lust.'

'I was thinking rather in terms of your mother's relationship at that time with your uncle, Clarence.'

'We were really too young and self-wrapped then. But we have wondered, specially these last few days.'

'Tell me what happened when Clarence arrived.'

'Well, we didn't really know who he was. It's twenty years, you see.'

'How did your mother take his return?'

'There was, I grieve to say, a blazing row. We heard it going on in the drawing room. We believe she threw things at him, because afterwards Fanny went in surreptitiously with a dustpan and brush and normally, she never clears up anything.'

'But the row didn't go on for two days?'

'Mama stayed in her rooms for the rest of the time.'

'Is that strange or not?'

'Well, for a couple of days, yes, it is. One day, sometimes, but we don't remember two — or nearly three.'

'And what was Clarence doing during that time?'

'He was mooning around in Father's old study. It's kept like a kind of museum, you know. Like the Heavenly Attic. I meant to mention that.'

'Do.'

'Well, that's where Mama keeps all Father's old treasures. Their secret treasures. What they are, nobody knows because it's kept locked with a weird sort of lock that has two keys.'

'And you think that Clarence might be in there?'

'It's a thought,' he admitted, watching me steadily.

I sat back and looked in the fire for a while.

'I'm not sure you've got a case here at all,' I said. 'There's a hat found beneath the river bank; Clarence was seen to come but not to go.'

'You've given an interesting picture of a — an unusual family, but that's all. I understood you, in the first place yesterday, to say that the matter was causing great alarm and it was a matter of urgency.'

'It is. I have kept this document in case you thought as you obviously do.'

He gave me an envelope. It contained a five pound note. I looked at it, turned it over and looked again, then stared at Ralph.

'Look at the troops issuing from Wellington's nose,' he said.

I looked again, very closely at the part indicated, and there was some very small writing interwined with the battle scene. 'Call dicks if U don't see me go. C.'

'That's very fine work,' I said, surprised.

'Uncle Clarence served his apprenticeship as a forger. That was one reason he went away all that time ago.'

'How did you get this?'

'He gave it to me as he used to when he gave me a tip as a small boy. He said, 'Study it, lad, and you may prosper.'

'So he went to this trouble when he was in the same house with you. Why?'

'If I knew the answers to these puzzles I wouldn't have called you, dear boy.'

'Did you tell any of the family?'

'Nary a soul. We don't trust each other to that extent. We each have our secrets, and keep them. The household is a closed shop and each member is close.'

Once again I looked in the fire and tried to sort out the Van Deken farrago in my mind.

'It's lunatic,' I said, turning back to him. 'There is just nothing to get hold of. Here was a man you hadn't seen for twenty years disappearing after two days and to find what happened you offer a thousand a week fee.'

It was my turn to lean on the table to look carefully at him.

'What exactly is the reason you must know what happened to him?'

'I would like to know Mama didn't do it,' he said gravely.

'Can it benefit you if she didn't?'

'Naturally. The image of one's mother must remain pure.'

'Really, Mr. Van Deken!' I said, with some contempt. 'You seem to have forgotten what you've been talking about all this time.'

'Mr. Ber — Gaunt,' he said, stumbling over names and almost missing his cue, 'I may talk of my mother as I wish, but nobody else can't.'

'Come now! That surely doesn't matter to the tune of a thousand pounds a week, however interesting the job might be to watch.'

He reached into his breast pocket and brought out a wallet which he laid on the table. He opened it and drew out a single cheque which he pushed across the table to me.

'A cheque on my bank — not me, in case you thought I was spoofing,' he said. 'That's for the first week. That cheque can't bounce, old boy, nor can it be stopped. It's as safe as the Bank, and it's for you, as you see.'

I am a normal person. I don't mind pushing my nose into a private nuthouse for the sort of money just passed to me, and it did help to overcome some of my scepticism about the story I had heard so far.

He suddenly put his hand out across the table.

'Done?' he said.

I shrugged, and shook hands.

'Come to dinner,' he said, getting up. 'Meet everybody. The meal may be stinking. It depends on what punishment Mama thinks we've earned today, but your coming might sway it towards the eatable.'

He did his coat up. 'Better ask them to put sandwiches in your room upstairs, in case you can't stomach the crap we get.'

'Supposing I am asked to stay?'

'Don't,' he said firmly. 'I want you to get into the house after eyeryone's abed and take a damn good look round. See what you can find.'

'Oh, is that it?'

He didn't take any notice of the remark but went on, 'I'll give you a signal out the window when they're all a-snore, and leave a door on the latch for you. Come to grub at seven.'

He went. I sat looking at the fire for a while and then decided I might as well take some sleep against the night to come. I laid along the seat of the pew and went to sleep.

I woke when something ticked my nose. Looking up I saw the daughter smiling and touching my nose with her finger. She laughed.

'Don't you want your bed, then?' she said.

'Just a snooze,' I said, sitting up. 'I

was tired. It's the sea air.'

'Comes in fine at low tide off the mud,' she said. 'Come. I'll show you the room. Have you no bags?'

'In the car. I'll fetch them later.'

I followed her upstairs and into a room looking out the back and over stables to the grounds of the great Van Deken house.

'Will you make me a sandwich for later?' I said.

'Sure. Me and the mattress makes a grand samwidge.' She laughed. 'Yes, but what of your supper, then?'

'I'm going to the house for dinner.'

'I'll get you double lot of samwidges,' she said. 'Them's mazed up there. You could get seaweed and all, they say. Seaweed, grass, straw patty. Terrible it is. Mr. Ralph sneaks in the back here for what he can get, tis so terrible.'

'Do the others come down, here too?'

'Sometimes, yes, but t'other night there was a new man come down, and he fell over or somethen, for the blood was pouring out his head, and he kept saying not to get doctor nor nothen, for 'twas but a scratch, but he used half the plaster in the tin I gived him.'

'Did you know him?'

'No. I didn't see him before. Said his name was Clarence. Soppy name, that.'

# 2

She went to the window and pointed out to the big white house, banked by elms to windward, as if the wind would always prevail in the southwest as it had done for centuries.

It showed like a paper house from the street lights in the town.

''Fore you goes there,' she said, 'you wants to know what to expect, I reckon. Should I call my friend.

'Who's that?'

'Mary. She worked there till 'bout three days ago, then she was give the boot. She knows more about the old woman then does anybody.'

The remark made me suspicious that this girl knew what I was there for, and I had till then merely let it be known I had some business with the big house, but not what.

'Is it necessary to know before one goes up there?' I said.

24

'You feel pretty queer if you don't,' she said, turning from looking at the house. ''Tis not like to go somewhere normal. When a man went to dinner last, she locked him up there till four in the marnen and then sent him out. He swore he'd never go there more.'

I looked suitably surprised. In fact I was surprised that what went on up there was openly known.

'Who was that?' I said.

'He was tryen to get her interested in a society for ghosts. I suppose he reckoned there were money in it — for the ghosts.' She laughed slyly.

'How did you get to know that?' I said, laughing at her little joke.

'Mary. I reckon you should meet her, for what she can tell you on where not to go wrong, for you seen Mr. Ralph Van Deken to lunch and he'm one to tell you how to get into trouble with the Lady more than what you'd do by yourself.'

'You think he'd pull my leg?'

'Pull 'em off when he'd had some gin and Dubonnet. Haves a half glass of gin and filled up with Dubonnet and then says, just put a twist of lemon on top, darling, I always likes it on top. He'll have a half dozen such and then rush out the back door and back to grass dinner. 'Tis hard to guess why he'd want to see two of his Mother.'

I chuckled. She was a sly wit, the landlord's daughter. I began to feel warm towards more than her promise of comfort.

'Do you know much about her yourself?'

'I knows the hearsay, but we had a judge stay here once and he said hearsay's no good. You wants to meet the person what's telling the lies in the first place. Then you can ask questions and sort it out. He was good, the judge. You'd never think an old man would — talk so saucy, if you meet me.'

'I do.'

I let her chatter on a bit without listening too much when she was not talking about the Van Dekens; she was then generalising and pleasing me by what she said rather than giving useful information.

The General, before the battle, gets

every bit of information which might help or hinder his plan of action. If I could sort out pride and prejudice from information in talking to Mary, it would be a shield at least against certain attacks from the woman I felt would try and batter down my efforts to find out what had happened to the luckless Clarence.

In fact, Mary had been sacked a few days after the disappearance of the long-lost step-brother, and might even give the key to what had happened to him. Or begun to happen to him, for she was hardly likely to have seen a crime take place.

'Well, if you think Mrs. Van Deken is really difficult, it might be a help to see your friend,' I said.

'I'll ring her now,' she said. 'She's the blacksmith's daughter.'

There was a residents' sitting room with a log fire in a wide brick fireplace. The girl, Mary, came within a few minutes of Annie going down to phone.

She was a tall girl with dark bobbed hair and fringe and wore a quite expensive looking wool cloak over black skirt and white shirt blouse.

'Annie said you wanted to talk about Mrs. Van D.,' she said. 'I just left there two days back.'

'You had a job there, didn't you?'

'I went as a lady's maid,' she said. 'Then it turned out I had to look after all the ladies — that's five. You know, look after their personal things.'

'How long were you there?'

'About a month, all told. It wasn't bad to start with. Once you get used to the idea they're all wild bonkers, you settle down to it. It all got very interesting. All, what they call, the cross plots.'

'Scheming?'

She laughed.

'That's mild. They seem to do nothing else but suspect each other of plotting to get one better with the old woman.'

'In order to do better in the Will?' I said.

'Yes, but I don't know it would make much difference,' she said. 'The stepbrother-in-law turned up suddenly one day and he sort of hinted to me that the money was in trust and Mrs. Van D.

lived on the interest. The rest of the money had already been split up between the children by the father years ago.'

'That's what he said?'

'That's what I thought he meant.'

'Why did he tell you such a thing?'

She smiled.

'He fancied me. I didn't mind him either. I think that's what gave the old woman the idea in the end.'

'The idea that made you leave?'

'Yes.'

'Do you mind telling me what that was?'

'Not a bit, no. She had me in one day — day before yesterday and said she was very anxious to keep her sons at home in her old age and so on, and she offered me bigger pay.'

'Well?'

'The idea was I would become the house whore and keep the sons at home.'

She laughed and so did I.

'You're not serious,' I said.

'I am,' she said. 'She's like some old queen. She thinks she can make anybody do anything.'

'So you took offence.'

'Look, I'm not a puritan. I like playing around when I like and with what fellow I like. I'll not be paid to be shoved into it.'

'Something must have given her the idea.'

'Oh yes. You know how it is when somebody like me comes into a house which offers nothing but Mum and sisters for the boys. The sisters noticed me getting pats on the bottom and little digs — you know. I don't have to tell you, I'm sure.

'Well, I made a joke of it all, but when Clarence turned up he was different. More a man of the world, and full of fun and — well, wicked, I suppose.

'Then the sisters noticed and told Fanny and Fanny and Mrs. Van D. got together and they hatched this idea and so I got interviewed with the proposition.'

'So you think it was Clarence who gave them the idea by his behaviour towards you.'

'It was a game of strip poker he challenged me to and he kept cheating,' she said. 'Then one of the sisters walked in to get a book. The game was over and I was just picking my clothes off the chair. Clarence was down to his pants.

'Well, Charlie — her name's Charlotte — sort of backed out and closed the door very quietly in case we hadn't noticed.'

'And then?'

'I said, 'What shall we do?' and Clarence said, 'Say nothing without your lawyer' and laughed. Then he said, 'Pardon me while I silence dear Charlie', and he went off with the pack of cards to find her.'

'Did he find her?'

'I don't know. I didn't see him any more.'

'That was the day he vanished?'

'Well, nobody saw him after.'

'He just disappeared without warning?'

'Yes. I was very surprised, because from what he'd said I shouldn't have thought he'd go.'

'What about the family?'

'They looked for him, but Mama just said he'd come uninvited and had gone the same way.'

'She didn't like him?'

'Mr. Gaunt, she doesn't like anybody. It's an awful thing to say about a person, I know, but she really doesn't. When I was there I used to think she really enjoyed not liking anybody; like a religion.'

'Yet you stood it for a month.'

'It was interesting. Like watching crocodiles and getting shivers thinking what it could do to you if it could get out.'

She did shiver slightly then and I saw her hands clasp with sudden tightness in her lap.

'Then when I saw more and more of what was going on I began to realise that it was worse than I thought.

'She wanted to trap everybody so they had to stay whether they wanted to or not. She wanted to make them do something so they'd be afraid to go.

'That's why she wanted to buy me for the sons. I'm sure that was it. It would have fixed me, wouldn't it? It meant if I left I'd have to go right away where nobody knew me if I wanted to get married, because that's the sort of thing she does.

'Half the stories that get out of the house she sends out herself. She traps people by making them afraid to go out. That's why her children stay.'

'But I thought she held them by making them think she'd change the Will if they went.'

'That's what it come to, I believe,' she said. 'But then Clarence came and if he said to the others what he said to me, then they were being scared for nothing.'

'But are you sure he knew that what he said was right?'

'He used to spoof but not about things he knew. I mean he was surprised when he heard she could change her Will and alter where the money went.'

'Then Clarence suddenly went away and nobody saw him go?'

'Yes.'

'And then Mrs. Van Deken offered you this — new position?'

'Yes.'

'She explained exactly what she meant you to do?'

'She did.'

'What was your immediate reaction?'

'I didn't believe it. I laughed.'

'What happened then?'

'She lost her wool. She bawled for Fanny and told me to get out and she'd have my bags thrown out after me.'

'Did you do that? Go straight away?'

'No, I went and packed. Ralph helped me downstairs and drove me home.'

★ ★ ★

The door opened. Annie brought in a tray of tea.

I said, 'Annie, which night did Mr. Clarence come in with a wound in his head?'

'A couple of nights back? Let me see, Wednesday I think — No. It was Tuesday. That's right. Tuesday.'

'Then Mrs. Van Deken made you that offer next day, Mary?' I said.

Mary was staring at Annie, surprised and I thought, angrily.

'You didn't say about that to me!' Mary said.

'He asked me not,' Annie said. 'Kept on about it wasn't worth botheren about. He tripped at the fence, he said.'

'Do you remember what time it was?' I said.

'Yes, sir. Roughly just after ten. We was still open. I mind that.'

I turned to Mary.

'What time did your card game finish on Tuesday?'

She looked into the fire.

'It was a funny night, if you know what I mean,' she said. 'Mrs. Van D. didn't feel good, she said, and we rushed dinner through and she went to her room on her own. Well, once she goes, they all break off.

'Mr. Clarence followed me and suggested this card game and the others was all gone to their rooms so I was game — ' she broke off then and almost laughed. 'I liked him, you see. He made me laugh.

'Well, so we played and all like I said. Then when he went to find Charlie I dressed and went to Mrs. Van D's room and knocked. She didn't answer and the door was locked.'

'Wasn't that unusual?' I said.

'Oh no. She'd do that to send everybody half mad thinking she'd done herself in, and then, after they all felt certain she had, she'd walk out. I reckon she listened, other side of door.'

'Did she open it eventually?'

'Sometimes. Not that night. The family had got used to the trick before I went there and didn't take any notice. I didn't see anybody, anyhow.'

'How long did you wait at the door?'

'Oh, I didn't. If you play up to her looney tricks you go nutty yourself. I went to bed.'

'So you didn't see any of the others?'

'Fanny came in my room later on.'

'The companion and housekeeper?'

'Yes. She was in a state. She said she wanted to talk to somebody or she'd go mad.'

'Fanny?' said the landlord's daughter, startled. 'What got at her? What did she say? Did she tell you?'

'Well, she said she'd had enough and was going to leave the next day. She was really put out. Cried and everything.

Look, I don't want it to get about, Annie. She's not that bad, when you get to know her. I think she has to pretend a lot for the old bag — Mrs. Van D., I mean.'

'I thought she and Mrs. was a couple of — ' Annie stopped herself. 'She didn't go, did she?'

'No. She was there next morning, just the same. Up to when I went, I mean.'

'Miss — er — Mary,' I said for up to then nobody had told me her name, 'what did Fanny talk about that night she went into your room? About the reason for her having had enough.'

'She said he'd been insulted and degraded and goodness knows what. I thought it was funny because I'd always thought she bossed the old woman as much as she bossed her, if you know what I mean.'

'But something happened that night to upset her?'

'I suppose it did, but the way she said it, I thought she was adding up a lot of scores from times before, if you know what I mean.'

'So she didn't say anything particular

had upset her that night?'

'Well, yes. It was Mrs going off from dinner like that. That seemed to frugle it — I mean, blow her nut for her.'

'Something Mrs. Van Deken said at dinner?'

'She and Fanny never spoke to each other at table. Mrs. was always telling the family off about one thing and another.'

'Even when Clarence was there?'

'Nothing makes any difference to Mrs. She lashes 'em. She really does. If she ever spoke to me like that I'd chuck the soup at her.'

'Grass soup?' I said.

'Well, I've heard about that, but never had any grass when I was there. She had a thing about puddens then. Need for more vitamins and filling-up, she said. Steak pudden, jam, treacle, ham, chicken — anything you can stuff in a pudden we had.'

'Curious.'

'No. Not that. It seems when they had grass her daughter Alex — that's Alexandra — said if she had any more grass she's be blown off with the wind she was so thin, so the puddens was to build it all up again. I tell you, they're as barmy as barn owls.'

By then we three had finished the tea, toast, cake, biscuits and celery.

'Tell me, Miss — um — have you any harsh feelings about Mrs. Van Deken? After all she did to you?'

She looked askance.

'Me? She didn't do anything to me. Not so I minded. I didn't give her the chance. Hard feelings, or no. I think of her as a nut case. Really I quite enjoyed myself while I was there. It was like one of those crazy films.'

She thought for a moment and I let her go on.

'Sometimes I thought the daughters were worse than the old woman,' she said and looked at me.

'In what way? Because of their scheming?'

'Well, they were always whispering and changing about. I mean, sometimes Charlie would be thick with Laura against Alex, and next week the other way about: Laura and Alex against Charlie. It got so you didn't know which plot was on and could give one the wrong message.

'Some times I used to think they did it to get me stewed up trying to work out what was going on.'

'They confided in you as their lady's maid?'

'They confided in me about what they personally thought of each other and that changed all the time. It got my head whizzing round sometimes.'

She shrugged as if the whole thing was really not worth trying to work out.

'What do you really think happened to Mr. Clarence?' I said.

She looked at me very quickly.

'I wouldn't like to guess that. There's always been talk about men who's called there and didn't come out, but it's come to be a sort of joke, like a bogey man thing.'

'But this time a man did call and stay and did disappear without saying he meant to go.'

'Yes, that's true, but — ' She was doubtful.

'You thought he'd be there next

morning, didn't you?'

'Well, yes. He hadn't said, and I think he would have been.'

'He came here, after he left your card game, bleeding from a wound in his head. How long did he stay?'

Annie said, 'He drank three treble Scotches and said that had given him strength to go back, and he went by the back as he come'd in. I told you. The people from the house always comes back way.'

'When did Mrs. Van Deken make the suggestion to you?' I said, looking back to Mary. 'At what time? Do you remember?'

'Well, 'twas just before lunch, but the meals are not always regular. It depends on who's having a row with somebody and that holds things up.'

'Was there a row that morning?'

'Oh yes. The daughters were banging it up proper, one way and the other. Arguing.'

'You don't know what it was about?'

'No, but I heard Ralph join in, too. I know his voice.'

'But not the younger brother?'

'Dudley? No. I don't know where he was. Don't remember seeing him that morning.'

'Who does the cleaning and cooking?'

'Oh, the daughters. That's why meals is irregular. Mrs. goes down and pokes her nose in every saucepan and that, but they do the actual work.'

'They keep the whole house clean?' I said incredulously.

'Oh no. There's a small firm comes in twice a week and cleans and sweeps everything. Very good they are. The boss pleases Mrs. I'd say. They always talk a long time after the women go with the van. The women who do the cleaning, that is.'

'That's all done by machines?'

'Oh yes. Place screams with 'em when they're at it. Mrs. marches up and down watching 'em. She said once they ought to strip to the buff, like men. I reckon she wanted to get a whip to their backs to make 'em go faster.'

'Do you think of her as a slave driver?'

'No. She likes to whip people, mostly

with her tongue or her ideas, or what she gives 'em to do. It's to make 'em wriggle more than make 'em work. She's a weird old bag, that.'

The point which impressed me about Mary was that although she clearly believed the old woman was evil, she showed no bitterness towards her. Almost as if she almost agreed with some of the eccentricity.

Suddenly she shot me a thunderbolt.

'What is it you're after?' she said sharply.

'Mr. Ralph asked me to help him.'

'About Mr. Clarence?'

'Yes.'

Annie got up and took the tray.

'I'd best take this down. 'Tis near openen' time for the bars.'

She went out. Mary picked up her gloves.

'Is there anything else you want to know? I don't mind,' she said.

'You've been very helpful,' I said.

'But what's it about — really?' she said, cocking her head.

'It's about trying to find out what

happened to Mr. Clarence,' I said.

'He might have gone on his own,' she said. 'But then, I think he would have come back. He liked a joke, but he liked it quick. He wouldn't have hung about all this time.'

'Then what do you really think happened?'

'They might have killed him,' she said slowly. 'But he was such a quick man, strong, too. I think he could stand up for himself against anybody there in that house.'

# 3

'Do you think it's possible he was murdered?' I said.

The girl stared at the fire for several seconds.

'I don't know,' she said. 'But I know this. Mr. Clarence wasn't a man to hide. He might go off by himself without saying anything to *them*.'

'You think he would have told you if he meant to go?'

'I'm sure he would. That's why I came here when Annie called me up. He's gone, I know that, and I don't feel good about it, but murder — I don't know about that. An accident, perhaps.'

'But would that family have kept quiet about an accident?'

'No. It's the last thing they'd do, really.'

There was a tap on the door, which then opened and Annie looked in.

'It's Miss Charlie from the house!' she

whispered. 'Wants to see Mr. Gaunt. Shall I let her up?'

'Let me get out first,' said Mary, also whispering.

'Use the other door. She's on the stairs now.'

Mary looked at me then nodded, whispered goodbye and left by a door in the recess on the right of the fireplace. Annie opened the landing door wide.

'It's Miss Van Deken,' she said loudly.

The daughter came in and Annie closed the door behind her. Charlie was, unexpectedly, I admit, a pretty girl in her late twenties. She was fair and inclined to plumpness. She wore trousers and a fur jacket which was then open showing a plain shirt well filled and a lot of necklaces all hanging together round her neck.

She introduced herself.

'Ralph told me you'd come,' she said, eyeing me as if to scan every detail of my features. 'About Clarence.'

I had come down to this place under the impression that Ralph would keep my real purpose quiet, but it began to look as if he had plastered it on the public notice

46

board in the church porch.

'I'm Charlotte Charlie,' she said. 'Don't mention it, I'll sit down.'

She did.

'There's been a kerfuffle up at our house,' she said, cocking her head at me. 'We had a visit from a long-lost Uncle and I think one of our lot murdered him.'

She said it quite calmly as if murder was a usual thing to happen before dinner at the Van Dekens'.

'Really?' I said, with mild interest. 'Did Ralph tell you I was an undertaker or something? I'm not, but I'd want commission for getting one suited to the circumstances. Such professional men are expensive.'

She watched me then with a sharp eye, not quite sure what to look for in my face.

'What did Ralph say to you?'

'He said he'd got you here to clear it up.'

'Has he told the rest of the family that?'

'Hell's bells, no!' She sat up straight

then. 'Ralph and I get on. There are times when we might cut each other's throats, but most of the time, no. We've always kept secrets from the rest of the family, being the youngest, perhaps.'

'You and Ralph?'

'My two sisters are older; George's thirty-three and Alex thirty-five.'

'And your other brother?'

'Dudley?' She fiddled with the beads of her necklaces. 'Nobody really knows how old he is. Mama won't say. It's one of her things. She always leaves something to keep you guessing and asking questions.'

'But surely it's difficult to keep such a thing hidden from a family?'

'We don't know where Dudley was born or when,' she said. 'Not knowing where makes it difficult, and he won't say. Mama and the late Van Deken travelled a lot, feeling cocoa beans in Africa and places. We were home with a Nanny and so on and when Dudley turned up he was a boy and might have been three, five or six.

'Between ourselves we did think he

might have been an error on Mama's part, but he isn't the colour of cocoa beans and he's too bloody minded and rude and selfish to be anything else but a true Van Deken.'

'You came to talk about your Uncle and tell me why you imagine somebody killed him.'

'He disappeared one night and he wasn't the sort to do that. Ralph found his hat floating in the river.'

'That's hardly enough, is it? Can you think of any possible motive for anyone there to kill him?'

'Sex,' Charlie said.

'But in what sense?'

'He'd been doing the maid, and Fanny. That got up Mama's nose — Fanny, not the maid. She's jealous of Fanny, you see, and I think she was jealous of Clarence because she wouldn't talk to him when she found out and shut herself up till he — went, whichever way he did go.'

'Considering he was only there a few days he seems to have been very busy.'

'Very. I was at first under the impression he was sleeping exclusively with me, which was very irritating when I found out the rest of it.'

She looked grave as if expecting me to sympathise at once with such suffering by deception.

'He was no relative bloodily, you know. Step. That's why he was so popular with us, but when I found out about my betrayal, I began to wonder if that was all. Mary and Fanny, I mean.'

'Miss Van Deken — ' I said.

'Oh, don't be weary with me,' she interrupted. 'But you can't trust my sisters, and after all Clarence was on holiday.'

'Oh, he was?' I said.

She laid her hand on mine as it rested on my knee.

'You're not against sex, are you?' she said, with some concern. 'You don't look it.'

'I'm all for it, but as far as human affairs are concerned it causes more trouble than any other desire, and probably more crime.

'What you are suggesting is that one of your sisters, your mother or Fanny was so fired up with jealousy it led to the murder of Clarence.'

'Yes.'

'But what about you?'

'Me?' She seemed surprised. 'I'm not jealous. I do it for my complexion.'

Not for the first time I felt I was entering some sort of wonderland where anything crazy was normal and anything else was dismissed.

'You had no feeling at all when you found out about the maid?'

'Not a bit. She's young and pretty. But when it came to Fanny — well, she's forty and should behave herself more, considering her position.'

'What is her position exactly?'

'I'm not sure, exactly. Mama and she are very thick, but Mama is a schemer and you can't get fun out of that doing it alone. I mean, it's no pleasure to be seen talking to yourself and laughing, is it? You must have somebody else to laugh as well.'

'Maybe. Now Miss Van Deken, what is it you want me to do? So far I've had a resume of the surface love life of the missing step-relative, which may or may not give a jealousy motive for a murder.

'My experience is that one woman who finds out about another might be so jealous as to murder in a rage, but when she finds out about three or four she might well consider whether her lover had not better see a psychiatrist.'

Charlie started to laugh.

'What did he talk about?' I said suddenly.

'Talk about?' She was surprised.

'When he was alone with you?'

'In bed? Well, what would you think he talked about?'

'Leaving that out. Did he talk about his outside interests? Where he'd been? What he'd been doing?'

'Oh, he'd been everywhere. Used to get society jobs.'

'What — an escort?'

'Oh, no. Judging beauty contests, you know — Miss Offshore Australia 1978 and that sort of thing, and broadcasting gossip on local stations.'

'In Australia?'

'In wherever he ran to from the last

one. He was a very amusing man, you know.'

He sounded more like a professional rake, and I suspected she did too, and that was why she liked him.

'Did you ask him to do something for you?' I said.

She was startled at that.

'Why?'

'Did you?'

'Such as what?'

'Such as interceding with your mother in some way or other?'

'Such as blackmailing her, do you mean?' she said, with that attitude she had already shown; that murder or blackmail were as normal as marmalade for breakfast. 'No. Blackmailing Mama would be like trying to get fourpence out of a Chieftain tank.'

'She's a difficult woman?'

I though I'd better get back to the girl's type of character assasination, since every time I tried a shock shot it was like firing into a sandbag much used to being shot at.

'Women are difficult when they feel

like it, Mr. Gaunt, and I don't believe that's your name, but anyhow, I must be going back to help with the cuisine, which is very haute on your account, but don't hurry; half eight will be in plenty of time as dinner's not till nine. Mama has been waiting for the pheasant's head to drop off, you see, and it didn't happen till five-forty — ' she got up and went to the door, ' — so, see you then and don't bother with pyjamas,' she said as she walked out without looking round.

The door almost closed then opened again and she put her head through for an instant.

'I think you're wrong. We're a Sex Museum, not a Black one.'

Then she was gone.

I thought that if she was an example of the oppressed family of the grande dame, then Mama must be a steamroller with rubber children.

★ ★ ★

Later dinner meant time to play with. I decided to go down into the bar and listen for any local gossip that might be in the air down there.

At that time I was beginning to wonder whether the whole thing was not some expensive joke on me, but I had a cheque which claimed my responsible nature, and I did not want to give it back.

It was, after all, a cheque on a bank and not a paper piece liable to change at some drawer's instant whim or lack of funds.

The bar was not busy. There were three fisher-looking men at the bar, leaning on it with their blue jersey sleeves rolled up, showing tattoo marks commemorating some allegiance to something or the other. One was chewing, two were smoking pipes, all were staring into blue smoke with impeccable vacuity.

The landlord was behind the bar, polishing glasses. He stopped to give me a drink, then went on polishing. The fishermen stared at nothing.

I went over to the fire and sat at a pew where I had slept that afternoon. I got out my diary and made a few notes until I was interrupted by something soft pushing against my side.

I looked round at a woman in a fur coat and a round fur hat and what looked like pyjamas, judging from what appeared in the gap of the open coat.

The landlord polished glasses, but he was looking through the bottoms at me and the dark lady with a kind of sardonic twist to his mouth.

'You are a Miss Van Deken,' I said sitting back against the pew.

'Georgina, but I was a Mrs. Granger for a while, so you're not entirely right. May I press you into getting me a large gin with just a thin slice of lemon in it?'

I fetched the drink for her and sat down again.

'It's not really for sale, you know,' she said, pleasantly.

I said, 'What isn't?'

'The family reputation,' she said, and smiled charmingly.

She was dark and attractive, like her younger sister, but — and save for the pyjamas — better groomed.

'I wasn't thinking of buying it,' I said.

'Ralph said you'd come to write a book about it,' she said, with a charming show of interest.

'Tell me, have you ever murdered your uncle?'

'Why on earth should I murder my uncle?' she said in beautiful surprise. 'I haven't got one.'

'You haven't? Then it's no use to my book. In my books everybody gets murdered, uncles in particular.'

'Oh, I love that kind,' she said, snuggling against my arm. 'Let me help you murder somebody. What about my ex-husband? He was a positive brute. He beat me.'

She almost pleaded for me to be sympathetic.

'What did you do about that?' I said.

'I liked it,' she said, sitting up and taking her glass. 'The trouble with him was he went broke, and if that isn't cruelty I don't know what is.' She sipped her drink. 'Otherwise I love everybody,' she said and pulled the coat apart so I could see a musical note embroidered on the left front. 'That is the breast which soothes the savage human,' she explained and closed the coat again. 'Tell me, what is your real name?'

'My real name?' I said, none too pleased.

'Well, book writers always use false names, don't they?'

'Tell me, Mrs. — Miss — '

'Call me George,' she said. 'May I ask you a question?'

'No, I'm asking you one first.'

'You're not supposed to be brutal to me.' She pouted.

'I am not being brutal to you. I am just going to ask why you came to see me here when you knew I was coming to dinner.'

She put her hand down and took a sharp grip of my upper right leg.

'You're pretty strong, aren't you?' she said, and let go.

'I asked you a question, George.'

'I came to ask you a very special question,' she said, bending close and almost whispering.

'Well?'

'Do you like malt whisky with pheasant

or do you prefer a Burgundy?' She was deadpan serious. 'Father always preferred Scotch.'

'What a question to come all this way for,' I said. 'Is that all?'

'I thought you were fussy about food and things,' she said, surprised.

'Who said?' I asked. I felt angry and looked towards the landlord, who was still polishing glasses.

'It's well known!' she said. 'It's in Who's Who.'

'Who do you think I am?' I asked.

She put her face close to mine and smiled, her eyes half shut.

'I don't know, but so beautiful,' she murmured, and grabbed my leg again.

I pushed her hand away and said, 'I shall have to be very cross with you, George.'

'And what will you do?' she said eagerly.

'I shall ask you what you've done with your uncle since you haven't got one now.'

'Oh!' she pointed at me as if she had just realised what I meant. 'You mean my pretend uncle. Well, I haven't got him. He's gone back to Brazil.'

'To Brazil?'

'He has a coffee mine in Brazil.'

'Ah, a coffee mine,' I said. 'That would be the Brazil where the coal grows on trees?'

'You are stupid,' she said. 'All the richest men have a coffee mine there. When the price goes down, you see, they stick all this coffee down an old disused mine till the price goes up again, then they dig it out. That's why they're rich.'

'I thought he came from Australia.'

'Oh, he does, too. He has a wool mine in Goolabongalong or somewhere.'

'When did he tell you this — ?' I began and then though, 'Oh hell! the answer's going to be, *in bed*!', so I went on, ' — or did you know it all?'

'I knew it, but it's secret, you see. He doesn't tell the others.'

'I understand. Did you see him off?'

'Oh no. He sees me off.'

'From where — ? Oh no, it doesn't matter, does it? Only Ralph said he'd disappeared. That's why I made a joke

60

about you murdering your uncle.'

'Oh, no, I didn't,' she said. 'Mama did.'

'Oh, Mama murdered him?'

'My dear man,' she put her hand on mine looked very earnest, 'she's always doing it.'

She looked so beautiful that I began to realise what the game must be. I was being seduced by the beauties of the family who were making fun of any idea that Clarence had been done in.

That's why they were coming one after the other, to keep up a game of making Ralph look a fool.

And perhaps also to try and make sure of what I had really come for.

'But I thought your mother was a gentle old lady,' I said.

'Mama,' she said, 'is an entertainingly wicked old bitch who does exactly what she likes because she can afford it and she can twist men round any finger she chooses for the occasion. You'll like her. Everybody does.'

'Everybody likes her?' I said, surprised.

'Of course, dear man. They have to.'

She grabbed my leg again. 'Well, thanks for the gin. I'll see you for din-din.' And she smiled and kissed me on the mouth, then got up, opened the coat so I could see the beauty of herself in silk pyjamas, then wrapped it snugly round her and walked briskly out, smiling at everyone who watched her go.

Bundles of fun, the Van Deken ladies. I wasn't so sure I wanted to go on with my job if it meant finding one of them guilty.

In short, I was being softened up and knew it and didn't much want to stop it. I began to realise that Uncle Clarence might have been not so much a philanderer as a victim of human response.

The landlord came over to take her glass.

'Fetching, aren't they?' he said as he went.

Annie came into the bar room and across to me, followed by the suddenly interested eyes of the silent fishermen.

'Would you like somethen before you go up?' she said.

'No thanks, Annie. It isn't grass tonight. It's pheasant.'

'Pheasant? My! You must be Somebody.' She laughed. 'Well, I'll put out the samwidges for later, just in case.'

She went across to the counter and exchanged banter with the men before going out again. Two of the men decided to play darts. I sat on by the fire thinking over what I had heard and all the time expecting the sudden appearance of the remainder of the Van Deken offspring, Dudley or Alex.

The landlord came over to put more logs on the fire.

'Looking you over, I reckon,' he said quietly, without looking round to me.

'Seems like it. Do they usually do this?'

'No. They'll come in for relief and a gulp of this or that, but don't talk to any but me or Annie or missus. You haven't seen missus. She's over to Bideford. Sister's took bad late this afternoon.'

He went back. More people started to come in and the room began to liven up with talk and laughter. At eight Annie brought in a roast sirloin, straight from the oven in its own gravy, and some home made white bread.

Landlord began to carve slices with expert care and dished the meat up on slices of bread. The money fairly rattled on the counter, and for five minutes he served nothing else but beef on bread.

At the end he speared a thin sliver on his carving fork and carried it across to me over a paper napkin. I took it in my fingers.

'This is one thing the Van D's will come down for,' he said. 'But I reckon they have something special tonight, by the look.'

He went back. I ate the beef, wiped my fingers, finished my drink and got up. I was at the bottom of the stairs to go up when Annie appeared in the kitchen doorway.

'You didn't bring your things in,' she said.

'I'd forgotten. Thanks.'

I went out to the park at the back and got my case from the car. The passage was empty when I went up the stairs to my room. I unpacked the immediate necessities, shut the rest up in the case and stowed it in the cupboard-wardrobe.

As I turned to go, there was a knock at the door and Annie showed up again.

'You're going up there, then?' she said, coming in and closing the door gently behind her.

'Now. Yes.'

'Last time Clarence left, nobody saw him more.'

She watched me with a curious light in her eyes.

'He may just have gone away. We don't know that.'

'Well, I know that he didn't.'

I stopped buttoning up my coat.

'How do you know? Did he tell you anything?'

'He said he would be back,' she said. 'And he wanted to come back. I know that.'

Not another bed for Clarence, for Heaven's sake? What kind of man was he? The Casanova of the Coffee Mines?

'What did he say?'

'He said he would be back early morning and would wait here the day until his lift turned up. That's what he said.'

'He meant to stay here till he went altogether?' I said. 'Why didn't you say that before?'

'I thought you'd not believe, because the lift never turned up nor did he.'

# 4

From the agonised look on the girl's face it looked as if Annie was really telling the truth.

'Was it arranged you should make contact with the lift?'

'I was to tell him to wait. Yes.'

'How was he supposed to make himself known?'

'He was to ask for Richard Melbourne. I was then to ask him to wait and give him a room up here to wait in.'

'And he never came.'

'No. Nobody ever turned up. I watched, you be sure of that.'

'And you didn't see Clarence any more after he dressed his wound?'

'No.'

'Didn't you think that perhaps he met the lift when they were both heading for this pub?'

'I did think that, but he said he would come back here.'

'Clarence?'

'Yes.'

I asked no more on that score, thinking that, as in the other cases I had already heard about, Clarence had had a personal reason for calling back, which was why Annie was so certain he would have come.

News of the lift itself increased the likelihood of Clarence's intention to go quickly and quietly away from the troublesome family of Van Deken.

'Did he give any time the lift was supposed to turn up — roughly?'

'Next evening, it was to be, but like I say, nobody did come.'

I looked at my watch.

'Thanks for telling me, Annie. I'd better get up to the house.'

'I'll put out your samwidges later.'

I thanked her and went down and out of the side door into the car park. There were quite a few cars there then. Mine was not locked because I had just been out to fetch my things.

When I got in a woman was sitting in the passenger's seat, looking at me.

'Alexandra Van Deken,' I said.

'How did you know?' she asked.

'You're the only lady left. I've seen Georgina and Charlotte already this evening. George, Charlie, Alex. All boys' names.'

'Mama is simply mad on men,' she said. 'She adores their names as well as everything else about them. Father must have had quite a job watching us and wondering.'

'You don't suggest you may be bogus heirs to the Van Deken millions?' I said, starting up.

'It's a wise child,' she said. 'But oh no, I wouldn't admit such a thing.'

'But you might about the others?'

'Mr. Gaunt, you are singularly forward. We're not introduced.'

'Then why did you get in my car?' I drove out into the road and turned right.

'Drive past the gates,' she said. 'I'll show you the back way. It's prettier.'

'Is it? How shall I know? It's dark.'

She laughed.

'Prettier for me,' she explained. 'I want to talk a little before we get there.'

'Who told you about me?'

'An uncle of mine.'

I started.

'What? Who?'

'Past the gates. Now follow the high wall along to a lane on the right, then turn down it,' she said calmly. 'My Uncle Clarence.'

'He told you I was coming?'

'Not exactly. He said that if he disappeared, you would appear. Sounds like a trick, doesn't it?' She laughed again.

'When did he tell you that?'

'The evening he finally went. Drive a little slowly. I am a nervous passenger. My late husband was a very bad driver.'

'I thought you were divorced?'

'Oh, somebody's been talking, I see. No. I murdered him.'

'Oh dear,' I said, mockingly. 'Why did you do that?'

'Mama didn't like him,' she said.

My mind was confused by these sisters. I found it difficult to remember which one had married in the first place and somehow I didn't think it was Alex.

Or was it?

I felt sure they were all together in organising a general confusion attack. They came one after the other; one, two, then three. Carefully timed. One didn't bump into the next. It had to be organised.

'Are you rich?' she said, in a friendly sort of way.

'Who is?'

'Mama is supposed to be. But she hands it out like a lady with no arms. Venus, you might say. That's how she lost her cuddlers, I expect. The beautiful of our sex are so often the meanest, haven't you found?'

'I just couldn't answer that. I never find any rich ones. Now, I am driving slowly alongside this great long wall. What have you got to say?'

'I'm not sure.'

'Surely you rehearsed it before you got in my car. Criminals always do.'

'Oh, you are a nice man!' she said, and laughed.

They all laughed, these sisters. They were as far as my imagined picture of three oppressed little mice as could have been.

'What I had in mind to say was to warn you off the grass,' she said quietly. 'About Clarence, I mean.'

'You don't want me to ask any questions about him?'

'It might not be wise.'

'Why not? Is Clarence an awful secret? The black sheep the family never mentions?'

'I mean that if you ask questions about what happened to him, you might get killed as well.'

'By whom?' I slowed down as a gate in the wall appeared in my headlights. 'Is this it?'

'No. It's a lot further on. It's a big place. By whom you say? By whom. Are you bananas or something? If I knew by whom I'd know by whom Clarence was done in.'

'What was your husband by profession?'

She looked at me sharply.

'That was a turnabout,' she said. 'I'd almost forgotten that subject . . . He was a trick motor cyclist. He used to ride over fourteen buses in a row. But he wasn't that good. There was always an ambulance waiting after the fourteenth bus.'

'I should have thought you would have chosen a professional man.'

'He was a professional man. A professional bloody fool.'

'And he was killed?'

'One night, when I was visiting mother, he hit the ambulance.'

'That's well known to be unlucky. I notice you put your alibi before his fate.'

'And Mama's alibi.'

'You didn't say she was here when you visited.'

'She wasn't.'

I sighed. 'I suppose she was driving the ambulance.'

'I am going to be thoroughly crossed off with you,' she said. 'If there is one thing I cannot stand it's a witty bugger.'

'You are a free speaking family, I've noticed.'

'I watch a lot of television. There is such a lot of time to waste in waiting. We are like nuns now, you know.'

'So you mean you're all waiting for your mother to die?'

'We need the money.'

'You are trying to make me think you're all mad. I don't believe it.'

'You should try living with Mama and her friend for a year or two.'

'Her friend? Do you mean the companion?'

'Fanny. Yes.'

'How old is you mother?'

'Fifty-five.'

'Sounds like a long wait for you.'

I drove very slowly, trying to work out just exactly what this onslaught by the Van Deken brood might mean. Either all the ladies were acting in concert, or singly, in which case there must be a very sharp string puller in the background.

'Anything can happen,' she said. 'Now, you turn right down this lane.'

I turned down the lane. We were still keeping alongside the high brick wall enclosing the Van Deken lands. High trees overhung the top.

'What was your Uncle Clarence's profession?'

She laughed.

'Anything that paid cash and a woman,' she said.

'A fortune hunter?'

'Oh no. A bon viveur.'

'A travelling man?'

'Restless as a flea. He'd never stay. Always moving on.'

'Did you see him the night he disappeared?'

'I told you I did.'

'Do you know what time?'

'It was about ten. He was coming to the front door with his hat on. I told him gentlemen didn't wear hats indoors. He said gentlemen with holes in their heads did.'

'What did you think he meant?'

'I asked him. He said he'd got a bash on the head with a marlinspike, whatever that is.'

'Did he tell you how he got hit?'

'No. I asked him what he'd done and he replied in Australian, and very improper it was. He was an outspoken man.'

'You speak of him in the past tense.

You believe he's dead?'

'I think he would have shown up if he wasn't.'

We came near some gates in the wall and I slowed to a crawl.

'Why would he have shown up?'

She hesitated.

'There was a little unfinished business,' she said. 'Yes it's through these gates. You just ease up and the gates will open. And they'll shut behind, as well.'

As predicted, the gates opened ahead of us and I drove through. In the mirror I saw them shut behind us.

We began to go down a badly metalled road through a wood.

'Could you tell me what was the unfinished business?'

'Well, as you ought to know, I suppose, he was due for some money for work he had done.'

'Work for you?'

She said nothing for a moment. We went sneaking down through the ghostly uprights of the wood. I began to think the trees might move again when we had gone by.

'I don't think I'd better tell you any more,' she said. 'I've told you the reason he should have come back. Don't push your luck. I have warned you. You could disappear. He did.'

★ ★ ★

As we rounded a bend in the long drive a man stepped out from behind some trees on a corner and waved to me to stop. He was a bit too near for me not to stop considering the width of the lane, so I obeyed.

He came round to my window.

'Will you give me a lift up to the house?'

I turned to glance at the woman beside me, but she wasn't there. Instead the nearside door was a little open.

She had slipped out, doubtless having noticed that, when she'd had got in, no interior light had come on at the opening of the door. Equally, she had guessed, it wouldn't come on when she slipped out in a hurry.

I have a switch to turn off the inside

lights as sometimes the customers I have like to be interviewed in a car but don't want to be seen getting in or out of it.

She had twigged that pretty quickly, which did not indicate a muddle-headed female.

I looked at the fellow at my window.

'Of course,' I said. 'I'm going up to dinner.'

'Oh,' he said. 'You're Mr. Gaunt. I'm Dudley Van Deken.'

He came round the front of the car, as if wary I might drive off and leave him, and got in the door Alex had left ajar.

We started off. At that point I had seen all the five children of the lurid Mama, one after the other, though this last one had almost spoilt the timing by treading on Alex's heels.

I didn't remember ever having a job to do which was unfolding step by step and spreading such a red carpet of lies, distortions and deliberately malicious suggestions before I had even got to the scene of the assumed crime as this one.

One after the other the plotters

appeared on the scene alone and gave his or her peculiar story without much regard for the details the others gave.

For instance, Ralph had said only one sister had been married, but Georgie and Alex said they had married. True — or said to be true — Alex was a widow, and Ralph may have been counting divorces only.

Then again, the story of the stunt husband seemed a bit wild though the children of the rich have been known to marry tramps for some obscure reason or the other.

Anyhow, here was Dudley, the last of the line, lying in wait amongst the trees as if Alex had previously tipped him off that she would bring me in by the back way.

Except that she had dodged out when he had appeared.

Every incident seemed to add two and two and make three and a half.

'What did you want to tell me?' I said.

'How did you know I wanted to tell you anything?'

'You do. You just said so. Come on. Let's have it. We can't be far from the house now.'

'You know Clarence was murdered?'

'Was he? How do you know?'

'Well, he disappeared and I'm sure he didn't mean to.'

'Right. You think somebody killed him. Who?'

'I don't know. We're a whole stackful of intriguers up at the house. Everybody's working on a plot of some kind or the other.'

'Including you?'

'No. I just sit around and hope for the best.'

'The best being that somebody else will strangle Mama?'

He hissed out breath.

'I say! That's a bit rough!' he said.

'What else do you sit around for?'

'I write poetry. Like Edgar Allen.'

'Poe? Poems about Murder? Haunting? Buried Alive? Rising of the rotting Dead? That sort of thing?'

'I have a lean to the macabre. Yes.'

The wood ended ahead and I could

see the house about a quarter of a mile ahead. I stopped and switched the lights off.

'What did you need to tell me? Come on! I must report for dinner.'

'I am sensitive to atmosphere.'

'A poet. Yes. One understands that. But what did you sense in the matter of Clarence?'

'There was an atmosphere when he turned up. A feeling of alarm at his coming.'

'Whose alarm?'

'My mother's. And her companion also added to the aura of desolation. I felt affected by it. I felt something evil was in train.'

'Did you feel Clarence had brought it?'

'No. The evil began when he arrived. As if something was waiting to snatch him, once he had been there only an hour.'

'Are you interested in psychic matters?'

'Not to the dead and gone, I believe, but to evil that is alive, and it came to life when Clarence came to the house.'

'Did you hear someone say something which gave you that idea, or was it a feeling of the atmosphere then?'

'Not words. The tone of voices, yes. The whispers, the tones of malice.'

'And you sensed this in your mother and her companion?'

'My sisters, also. A distaff lay, you might say.'

'Are your sisters malicious?'

'To a degree — yes.'

'You felt they were hostile towards Clarence?'

'Not openly. Secretly.'

'Why not openly?'

'They were sweet to his face.'

'Wasn't your mother?'

'She was angry, I felt. Angry.'

'And the companion, Fanny?'

'Contemptuously hostile.'

'All in all, it was a damn bad atmosphere?'

'As you put it that way — yes.'

'But what about your brother, Ralph?'

'He made all the women mad by being right in with Clarence. They got on well. No hostility.'

'Ralph gets on with all of you, does he?'

'The girls always make a fuss of him. They always did.'

'But not of you?' I remembered the tattle about Dudley being a mystery addition to the family.

'Sometimes, and often not,' he said, staring ahead at the lights of the house. 'There has always been a suggestion that I am not quite a van Deken. Not a foundling, you understand. Mama is my mother all right.'

'I see. But that isn't my affair,' I said. 'How did you get on with Clarence?'

'Oh, he tried to twit me out of my melancholy,' he said. 'Didn't think too much of poets. Look — ' he opened his door. 'I want to show you something. I've got a torch.'

We got out. He turned to go right, into the wood. It was not that dark. The reddish glow from the town lights made the tree trunks shine eerily and just showed up bushes round which Dudley skirted.

He walked quickly, turning and twisting

83

in amongst the trees so that he almost disappeared in the shadows cast by the trees.

We went in quite a way before he switched on the torth.

The beam swung about over the ground like something solid. The way he walked made me think he had almost forgotten I was behind him.

Then in amongst a clump of birch trees there was a great pile of leaves, twigs and other debris which had been gathered from the wood by a forester.

He stopped by it. I came up with him.

'Funny place for a compost heap,' I said.

'Look,' he said. 'Don't touch anything, but look.'

The circle of the light haloed a shoe sticking out from the bottom of the heap.

As he asked, I didn't touch it.

It was a good shoe. I could tell that. It was a very good shoe, and worn.

'It's Clarence's,' he said in a dull voice. 'I think you'll agree, a live man could not lie with his foot at that angle.'

'When was this heap made?'

'Last week when they were clearing things a bit.'

'Have you disturbed it?'

'No.'

'When did you find this?'

'This afternoon. Late.'

'You believe Clarence has been under this pile since he was murdered?'

'What else?'

'Kindly give me the torch.'

He gave it to me and I shone it carefully round the heap.

'And the heap was made last week?'

'Yes. They keep the woods right for pheasants, partridges. Disgusting. Cannibalism.'

'The heap hasn't been disturbed since it was piled,' I said, and bent down.

'Don't touch it! For the lord's sake! I don't want to see — ' He turned his head away.

I picked up the empty shoe and held it under his ear.

'Look,' I said. 'It's empty. It's just a shoe.'

Slowly he unfroze and turned his head.

'A shoe,' he said, in a frightened whisper. 'Just a shoe. Like the hat.'

'Like the hat,' I said.

'But it's Clarence's shoe!' he said, almost angrily. 'I know that!'

'It's Clarence's shoe,' I said. 'And it was Clarence's hat in the river. Did he arrive with luggage?'

'He had a case, as far as I saw. It was a small case. He couldn't have had much in it. Oh yes!'

'Yes? What?'

He snapped his fingers.

'Somebody said, 'Thank goodness; he won't be here long'. I remember that.'

'Because of the small case. I see. Who said that?'

'Fanny,' he said, and put a hand to his forehead. 'Was it? I'm not sure.'

'You think Fanny's most likely to have said it?'

'Yes. I suppose I do.'

'She didn't like him?'

'She doesn't like anybody who gets near Mama.'

'You don't think she was attracted to him?'

'You mean jealous she couldn't outdo Mama? You could be right there.'

'Your first remark about her gave the impression she was jealous from a feminine angle.'

'Oh, I see. Well, yes. That could be. But she could have been jealous the other way as well. Fanny is an allsex person and jealous all ways as well.'

'Do you think she might have killed Clarence?'

'I don't think she would have done it herself, but she might have pushed Mama into doing it.'

I shone the torch round the area in which the heap stood, looking very carefully for any sign of a visit which had been repaired after, but saw nothing.

'Clarence's hat, Clarence's shoe,' Dudley said, as if trying to make up a poem. 'But where is Clarence?'

He looked up at me, and slowly shook his head.

# 5

'What does it mean?' Dudley van Deken said.

I finished shining the torchlight round the heap of leaves and switched off.

'It means Clarence has one shoe and no hat,' I said. 'No body was dragged to that heap, as you can see if you care to shine the light around. It looks as if shoe and hat were left around to create a worrying impression.'

'Don't you think he's dead?'

'All your family have told me he is, but a hat and a shoe and private opinions don't really add up to a certainty.'

'Then where is he?'

'All I can say he's nowhere you've looked,' I said. 'You have looked, haven't you?'

'I'm not just imagining that, because his name is Marley, he's bound to be dead as a doornail,' he said sharply.

'*Have* you looked?'

'I suppose we all have, but without telling the others. Our family is like that.'

'You have suggested, in one way and another that one of these family members didn't need to look.'

'They hid him, you mean? The guilty one? Yes.'

'You are a sensitive person. Aren't you outraged by the thought of one of your family being taken for murder?'

He thought for quite a few seconds.

'Yes — and then for other reasons, no. You may begin to understand when you've been to the house.'

'I think I'd better go there now.'

'Yes, well — You've set one fear of mine at rest, Mr. Gaunt. Let's get back to the house. Or rather — '

We started to walk, but he stopped then. I did too, and turned.

'What's the matter?'

'I think it best if you went alone.'

'Very well.'

I went on to the car. Dudley's decision to go alone was in keeping with the secrecy of the rest of the family — at least, that part of it which was put on for outside viewing. He just didn't want the others to know he had spoken to me.

It wasn't worth telling him that Alex knew he had stopped me. I'd no doubt he would find out.

As I went up the steps the front door opened. A man in butler's dress stood there to welcome me, correct, even down to white cotton gloves.

'Good evening, sir. Mr. Gaunt? Allow me to take your coat.'

He helped it off me, then as I turned he held it up, read the tailor's label, bundled up the coat and flung it to the floor in a corner of the hall.

'If you would follow me, sir?' he said, going politely ahead of me.

No one had mentioned a butler in the house, not even an eccentric comedian of a butler.

'What tailor do you recommend?' I said.

He stopped and turned slowly to face me.

'There are no good tailors, now, sir,

because the cutters are all part-time sheep-shearers and therefore good fit has become a thing of the past, sir, rueful though it is. Like Corbanders, sir.'

He opened a big white painted door.

'If you would be so good, sir, as to venture in?'

I went into a Victorian drawing room, lush, opulent, velvet and satin luxury. A variety of plump nude nymphs held up lamps, clocks, small tables and finally supported the arch at the end of the room, though those two were larger and plumper and someone had left a lady's umbrella hanging from the left hand nymph's left nipple.

The arch seemed to lead into a conservatory through a pair of glass doors.

'Would you care for a sherry, sir? There's none really good, I'm afraid, it all being slightly above the cooking range of fortified wines, however, if you wish — ?'

'No, thanks.'

'Very good choice, sir.'

I hoped to shake him.

'I am expecting to see Mr. Clarence,' I said.

He stopped, his back to me, then slowly turned to show his face.

'Mr. Clarence left, sir. So I understand. I am temporary. Just for the evening. Butler Rent, sir, if you have need at any time — ?'

'Not at present, thank you.'

He went out and closed the door. It looked as if he had been rented in my honour, as there had been no indication that any other guests were expected that night.

I looked at my watch, then at the clock on the mantle which was a gilt affair in the glass dome which housed a cherub swinging on the pendulum. It was four and a quarter hours fast.

As I stood there I heard the door open softly, and then shut again. The butler was having a look at what I was doing.

There were a few magazines lying about, mostly women's fashion glossies and free handouts from the Sunday papers. I went to the glass doors under the arch and looked through at what looked like an over-grown collection of tropical plants.

The door opened again.

'If the gentleman pleases — ?' The butler seemed to speak in half unfinished questions.

He made a sweeping gesture for me to pass him and go out. I went out. He followed quickly behind and went ahead of me to fling open another big white door. He again made a gesture of sweeping me through.

I wondered what crackpot establishment had taken on this pantomime artist to hire out, and went through into a very large room with a wide half arch at the end of it and a laid out dining room beyond it.

But in the first great room were the ladies.

I am not easily taken aback, but I certainly was on seeing the Van Deken feminine ensemble.

They were all in glorious Victorian dinner dresses, each a different colour, their half exposed bosoms luscious as peaches.

Rich ribbons, satins and velvet bows were brilliant in the lights. Mama was in the middle and the three daughters were gathered round her, one in front and one to each side, each in a curtsey, smiling, spread fans to their cheeks. It was quite beautiful, and Mama appeared to be quite as beautiful as any of her daughters.

She smiled in welcome. The daughters rose and moved to one side, still smiling at me. Mama held out her hand for me to kiss as I approached. I kissed it. She indicated her daughters with her folded fan, saying their names as she pointed to each.

By that time I felt almost certain I was the victim of some grand hoax, except that I couldn't imagine the wonderful period dress being brought in for a one night performance.

'Let us to dinner,' said Mama.

As she said that the butler hurried up to her side and hissed.

'I'm supposed to announce it!'

Mama smacked him across with face with her fan.

'Go about your business, Grayson,' she said, 'Outside.'

He went back and stood to attention to let her turn and go towards the dinner table.

Mama turned, and I was practically blinded by the surprise.

The fine dress was only a half one. As Mama turned she showed a completely naked back from her necklace to her shoes. In that surprising state she walked majestically into the dining room.

The daughters smiled graciously at me, then they turned, revealing themselves like their Mama. None took the least notice or took a glance at me to see my expression over these surprises.

They sat down at the mahogany table with it's silver and candles and Mama indicated me to sit on her right. I did so, wondering where the sons were.

'My late husband so liked a friendly joke,' said Mama to me. 'As did dear Clarence, but one had to be so careful that when one turned round he didn't get into the dress with you. He was humorous in his own right.'

'Is he dead like your husband?'

'Now that is a delicate question,' said Mama, thoughtfully. 'He disappeared a short while back. Disappeared from this very house. He was frightened I would ask him to marry me.'

She smiled graciously.

'Why should he be frightened of that?' I said, smiling.

She was very beautiful and seemed hardly old enough to be the mother of the three women at the table, but I didn't think their relationship was false.

'Tell me, Mr. Gaunt, what is your business?' she said, laying her hand on mine.

'I'm an insurance investigator,' I said. 'I look into doubtful claims. I'm on holiday at present. Your son Ralph invited me.'

The daughters were watching me without making much of it, and I hoped fervently that Mama did not know as much as they.

The butler came in with a trolley and soup tureen and proceeded to serve soup. He was not good at it and poured half of Mama's down the front of her dress — or half dress.

'You insufferable dolt!' said Mama. 'You've soaked my dress through!'

She waved his apologies aside, unfastened the dress below her bare shoulders, then folded the top part down into her lap and, with her great bare breasts commanding the table, she continued to talk to me as if nothing had happened of note.

'How did you meet my son, Mr. Gaunt?'

'I met him in the town,' I said, trying not to look at the mighty exhibition. 'He suggested I might come up. I hope he's well?' I looked at the empty places at table.

'Oh they come when they please. Vulgar, both of them. No manners at all. One would think they'd got the dinner ready and dressed by now.'

'Oh they're cooking?'

'They are trying. Usually the girls do it, but I decided it was the boys' turn. Dudley was late. I dare say his sauce will be all lumps.'

The butler went round with the soup.

The daughters took care where he was putting it. His handling of the plates was unsteady, and it was then I decided that the dolt was drunk.

When it was my turn I watched the shallow plate swaying towards me with great care, but after some weird attempts at landing, it came down safely.

'I wish you would do something for me, Mr. Gaunt,' Mama said when the butler had retired.

'Of course,' I said.

'The point is, we all believe my step-brother-in-law is dead, and I would like to make sure I did not kill him. I mean, I want you to convince my children of that.'

So she did know what I'd come for, the same as all the others.

Clarence. Clarence had feared murder, or something near it and he had told Ralph of me and what to do if he disappeared.

But Clarence, while leaping from one bed to another, must have given similar advice as he had sprung to and fro.

'But why do you all think he's dead?' I

said. 'Where did that idea come from?'

'Morbidity,' said Alex.

'He disappeared,' said Georgie. 'And we found his hat.'

'Also he did think of it himself, as if he knew,' said Charley.

'You see?' said Mama. 'And the boys think the same.'

'But finding a hat is nothing. People do slide off on their own without telling anyone,' I said. 'The important thing for any kind of crime is — do you know of any motive for anyone committing murder on this person?'

'Motive?' said Mama, surprised. 'Van Dekens have no motives. They are all crazy. Did no one warn you?'

'But crazy people have reasons,' I said. 'All that's crazy about them is they don't conform. Think of whether there is a motive, or a crazy reason, for killing Clarence.'

Mama clapped her hands together.

'You are marvellous!' she cried, eyes alight and bosom plainly quivering.

★ ★ ★

The women avoided my suggestion and talked for a minute or two about why the boys were taking so long, and what had happened to the butler, also being so long in serving.

I put in a word or two here and there, where it didn't matter, and thought about my position.

It was hardly a position at all. Asked, confidentially, to help in tracing Clarence, suspected murdered, I now found myself surrounded by every member of the household knowing what I had come for.

This meant that the guilty one knew as well as anybody else.

Further, the guilty one must be on very close terms with the innocent, and either he was already known for what he had done or was extremely clever.

It is one thing to bamboozle strangers and quite another to fool those who know you so well that there is no need for them to suspect. They only have to guess what's happened and then look for the least wrong flicker of an eyelid to be sure.

Specially within a family like this, who lived closely together, criticising each other constantly.

Either they knew already and weren't saying, or the villain was not in the family at all.

The third possibility, that Clarence was not dead, was on, but only just. Erratic, his career might have been, but there seemed little reason to bolt, leaving notes around suggesting he might be done in.

Nor would a man like Ralph be taken in to the extent of paying a thousand pounds in advance, and more each week, on a hoax.

He had paid it because he had been frightened that Clarence's death might be heaped on him.

It was a pity he did not turn up for dinner in time to start the proceedings.

The butler came back trundling the serving trolley, but hit the doorpost with a great crash and tinkle of offended chinaware. He said something very rude, thinking it to be sotto voce, and the ladies started talking louder.

He came in and began to hand out

the servings of pheasant which Ralph appeared to have carved out in the kitchen. He shot one serving right into Alex's lap and stood there nonplussed, wondering what had happened to the pheasant as he still held the plate.

She got up, smacked him across the cheek with her fan, hissed something in his ear and then stalked out in as dignified a manner as possible, considering her appearance from the back.

Unruffled, the butler completed serving and shoved the trolley out again.

'Didn't ought to have to serve as well!' he shouted from somewhere outside.

My plate gave off a strong aroma of high pheasant apparently simmered in port and Scotch whisky.

'They are trying to make me mad, Mr. Gaunt,' Mama said, with a certain sharpness of voice.

'Don't apologise, please,' I said. 'But where did you get that butler?'

'He is a chauffeur Clarence recommended. Clarence was a great humorist.'

Georgie took a bite of pheasant.

'What genius,' she said, with a snort.

'Who thought this one up? What's all this booze it's floating in?'

At that moment a tall, big built woman walked in from the doorway the butler had used. She went straight to Mama and put something on the table beside her plate.

'It's a watch,' said Mama. 'A dirty watch.' She looked up. 'Well, Fanny? Why?'

'It's Mr. Clarence's watch,' said Fanny. 'I saw him wearing it when he was here. Why are you dressed like that?'

'Well? Where was it?'

'It must have been out in the coke store. In the coke. I took the hod out and dug it into the coke pile and when I came back I saw this glittering in the coke. Just saw it in time. I almost put it in the cooker.'

'What do you think of that, Mr. Gaunt?' Mama said, turning and handing me the watch.

I looked at the tall woman.

'You fill the cooker from the top or straight into the fire door?'

'The top. I saw the watch as it slid

103

out with the coke. I just tilted the hod black in time, otherwise it would have gone in.'

'So it was well mixed up in the coke.'

'Yes.'

'It was taken off the wearer,' I said. 'The bracelet's intact. It's stopped at two-ten. That might be a.m. or p.m. The jerking it's just had has started it going again. When was the last delivery of coke?'

'Oh — September,' said Fanny.

This was the third personal item of Clarence's which had turned up since his disappearance. A hat, one shoe, his watch, dirty but undamaged apart from coke scratches.

'May I look in this coke shed?'

'Of course,' Mama said, warmly and patted my hand. 'But later. There is no hurry. Clarence has been gone two days now.'

'No hurry, of course,' I said. 'Quite impossible to shovel enough coke aside to bury a corpse in it. One person could never do it. You may have noticed how the stuff rolls back down the slopes,' I added, looking at Fanny.

Fanny smiled back sweetly.

'Sit down, Fan,' said Mama. 'Eat something. Call that numbskull to bring you your dinner.'

Whereupon Fanny brought out a screwed up hankie from her skirt pocket and burst into tears. She turned away.

'I can't bear to — Not now he's — ' Then she almost ran out of the room.

'Takes everything so personally,' Mama told me, confidentially.

I thought I would reverse the order of battle and attack the aggressors.

'You want me to find out what happened to Clarence?'

'We should love you to do that,' said Mama.

'We want you to,' said Georgie.

Charlie was busy tipping her plate and pouring her gravy into her wineglass.

'Yes, yes. Bravo,' she said.

'Right. I must have absolute freedom to go anywhere I want in this house.'

'It is yours,' said Mama, dramatically.

'Are there any rooms you haven't

looked into for some time?' I said.

'Well, there's my old treasure room,' said Mama. 'It just contains favourite things of my late husband's. All the other rooms are done by the cleaners.'

'I'll start there, in the treasure room,' I said. 'The first thing I have to be sure of, is that Clarence is not still here.'

'How grisly,' said Charlie, still tipping her plate over the glass.

Alex came back in modern evening dress, looking beautiful as intended.

'I have just been to my room,' she said, halting at the end of the table. 'And someone is knocking on the ceiling.'

'From the treasure room?' said Mama, very startled.

'Well, it must be, mustn't it?' said Alex. 'That's right above mine.'

'Sit down,' said Mama, sharply. 'Don't disturb the party.'

'But, my dearest, autocratic, bloody-minded, synthetic Mama,' said Alex, 'I am telling you somebody is alive up there!'

Ralph marched in from the kitchen.

'Oh shut up, Alex,' he said. 'You've

had knocks on the ceiling for years. It's the water pipes.'

Before Alex could snap out an answer, Dudley came in behind Ralph.

'Shut up, Alex,' Dudley said, seconding his brother. 'You know damn well he's up there. What I came to say is something has gone wrong with the soufflé. Could you help me, Mama? Fanny's gone liquid. Tears all over my cooker. Steam everywhere. Why don't you get rid of that moron?'

'One day, my favourite younger son,' said Mama, rising in half her magnificence, 'I shall murder you, and I hope I make a pretty picture with my head in a black bag.'

'They don't hang people now,' said Dudley, irritably.

'Then I shall wait till they do,' said Mama. 'Call the impossible waiter to bring your supper.'

'It's quicker to get it,' said Ralph. 'He's been soaking up the sherry so when he bends over it spills out of his ears.'

He went out again.

'Tell me, why did you both come in?'

asked Mama. 'Had you some reason?'
She eyed Dudley with some suspicion.

'I came in after Ralph,' he said. 'I
thought we'd sit down and get our dinner
served. I thought we'd force that layabout
to do his job for once.'

'Did you tell him to?' said Georgie
slyly.

'Who ever heard of Dudley telling
anybody anything?' said Alex angrily. 'A
weak willed pimple he's always been — '

Ralph called something from the
kitchen far away.

'Oh hell, something's caught fire again,'
said Dudley and went out shouting, 'All
right, I'm coming!'

'They never agree,' said Mama shortly.
'I've often — '

Dudley came running back.

'Quick! Where's that — ? Mr. Gaunt!
Come with me, quickly! You women stay
where you are!'

'Whatever — ' began Mama.

'Just Mr. Gaunt, and shut up the rest
of you,' said Dudley, and turned back
towards the kitchen as I got up.

# 6

I followed Dudley out of the dining room and down the passage to the kitchen. As we went, he spoke in a very agitated manner.

'Somebody's murdered that bloody butler,' he said.

'They didn't have a lot of time,' I said. 'Where is he?'

'In the kitchen. Ralph's keeping guard, a bit late in the day.'

We entered the big kitchen fitted with every sort of copperware, an Aga cooker and a big scrubbed wooden table with fine wooden pastry tools lying there, amongst other things.

One of those other things was the butler who lay there on his back with his lower legs hanging over the edge. It looked as if he had been sitting on the edge of the table when struck down.

Ralph looked up as we came in.

'I think he's dead — dead drunk,' he

said, frowning. 'He has been at the sherry more than somewhat. He's breathing now. Look.'

I had a close look at the drunken butler. He was breathing and exhaling an almost intoxicating aroma.

'Thank the lord!' Dudley said. 'We don't want any more corpses.'

'We haven't had one yet!' said Ralph angrily.

I lifted the butler's head an inch. There was a little blood on the wood table.

'He's been coshed,' I said. 'Better get a doctor.'

'No need. Fanny took first-aid lessons. She's good.'

'The man might have a broken skull.'

'Shouldn't think that'd affect his brain much,' said Dudley.

I thought he was somewhat disappointed the man wasn't dead. As butlers went, Grayson would be no loss, but being human in some respects there would be all the complications of police and coroner and so on.

'Fetch Fanny,' I said.

'Where is she?' Ralph said.

'She disappeared in floods,' said Dudley. 'I suppose to her room. I'll go and see.'

He went out. Mama came in just after, still wearing the half-dress but with a small tablecloth draped over her shoulders, the lace edges pinned together with silver sugar tongs in front.

'Well, is he dead or can he go on serving?' she said. 'The man's been nothing but a waste of money and time. Look at him now! That table top will have to be washed off.'

'He's been biffed on the head, Mama,' Ralph said. 'He's not well.'

'Fetch Fanny,' said Mama, waving her fan at the door. 'I had her trained as a nurse in case of need. She'll soon get him working again.'

'He's knocked out, Mrs. Van Deken,' I said. 'He won't work again tonight. He may have a cracked skull, which means hospital.'

'I think it was cracked before,' said Mama firmly.

Fanny came in with Dudley behind her. She went straight to the table and began to examine the patient. She was quite professional, looking at the eyes and for other signs of severe concussion.

There was a number of possible weapons on the table; two large wooden rolling pins and a meat flattener amongst them.

The main question was who had sloshed him, and what on earth for? This paragon of arrogant inefficiency was no member of the family, but a chauffeur from a rental firm whom Clarence had jokingly recommended as an emergency butler.

The attack was idiotic in any case, for it had to be discovered within a minute or two.

'Mrs. Van Deken,' I said, 'when did you take on this man?

'I phoned the agency Clarence recommended and named the man, as he'd said. So the man turned up about five. He explained that he was, in fact, a chauffeur, but that in the emergency — it was one, when I saw I'd got the wrong tradesman — and I stated my displeasure, whereupon he said he could buttle on his head. Which is what he seems to have done.'

Fanny straightened.

'A bowl of hot water,' she said imperiously.

Dudley went off and fetched one. Fanny had brought her own tin first aid box.

'Nothing's broken,' she said, as Dudley brought the bowl. 'I think the wallop, added to wallop, put him out.'

It was surprising to hear pub humour from such a very straight face.

'Well, he can't lie there,' said Mama. 'Get him on the sofa in the little room next door. After that,' she went on looking round at the assembled faces, 'we'll decide who did it.'

When Fanny had gone out with the stretcherbearers, Ralph and Dudley, I asked Mama a question.

'Have you a great many valuables in the house?'

'A fair number. As a matter of fact we have an annual row with the insurance people. They think I ought to bank some of it.'

'And money?'

'There is about five-thousand pounds kept here. A safe in my room.'

'Have you ever been burgled?'

'There are too many interested persons in the house,' she said with gentle irony. 'It would be an unfortunate burglar who ran foul of my children's greedy expectations. My family needs no burglar alarm, Mr. Gaunt.' She smiled.

'Did they think the butler might be a burglar?'

She was surprised.

'Oh! You think you have the motive already,' she said. 'Yes, the family were the only ones in the house beside that extraordinary man and yourself.'

I switched subjects.

'Do you really think Clarence was murdered?'

Her eyes moved slowly until she stared directly at me.

'I think he was, but I have no idea of what the motive could have been. None at all.'

'Had he any money?'

'He made a living, I believe. Specialist jobs. Pianist in a brothel. That sort of work. He was a very naughty man and everybody loved him, so long as they were female.'

She watched me with a glint in her eye.

'If you are thinking that he was caught in the act of trying to steal from me, please forget it,' she said. 'He would never have stolen from me. We were very fond of each other.'

She turned without another word and walked back to the dining room.

'Mr. Gaunt has had no food,' she said to her daughters. 'Get him some supper that's hot.'

'Please don't worry,' I said.

She went regally to the door, regal even with her back bare but for the tablecloth at the shoulders.

'And he has particularly asked for strychnine sauce,' she said, and went out.

Alex looked at me.

'You must be careful that your persona does not become non grata,' she said. 'That would not do.'

I went to the table and sat down with them.

'Now you all know what I was bamboozled into coming here to do,' I said. 'Clarence Marley is dead, as the doornail. Everybody here knows that. Each one of the inmates has told me that they know he is dead and that he was murdered.

'The only figment of evidence is provided by a hat, a shoe and a watch, which, lumped together, amount to Fanny Adams or less. That is all there is, and, perhaps, several accusations of broken promises — or expectations to make his acts less binding.

'That is all we have. Yet everybody here tells me he has been murdered, and everybody says they *know* he has. They don't think he has. They don't believe he has. There's no doubt at all: They know he has. You, you and you, and your brothers and your mother all *know* he was murdered.'

They watched me with a pretty interest. I thought they should have said something. They didn't. They waited for me to go on.

'Yes,' said Georgie.

'How do you know?' I said, and looked from one to the other of their attentive faces.

None spoke.

'Have you seen the body?' I said.

Again there was silence.

I got up. I was angry. I had been hauled down here on some joker's line and wasted hours listening to parts of a family I thought had been genuinely disturbed by a killing in their midst.

Now I was being treated as some kind of curio who thought that murder might be of some importance in the scheme of things instead of a subject for a light after-dinner laugh.

'I don't believe there is a body,' I said. 'I don't believe Clarence is dead. I believe he got fed up to the back teeth with your stupid intrigues and jealousies and just departed in the night. That, I think, is the truth of the matter and you are stirring this murder idea up so as to get him collared and brought back to face a charge of creating a public nuisance.'

The ladies at each other and then started laughing.

Before I could say what I felt like saying, Ralph came marching in from the kitchen.

'What the hell is there to laugh at?' he demanded.

They stopped laughing.

'I'm afraid Mr. Gaunt said it so suddenly,' said Charlie. 'And better to laugh than scream.'

'Said what?'

'That we had seen the body,' she explained.

'Oh,' said Ralph, and looked momentarily blank.

\* \* \*

I sat down again. So did Ralph.

'Where is it?' I said.

'I don't know now,' said Ralph.

'First: you have seen it?'

'Yes.'

'And you are sure it was Clarence's?'

'Yes.

'Then why don't you know where it is?'

They all watched me, wondering

who would answer. Alex proved the courageous one in the end.

'It was moved.'

'Where was it before it was moved?'

'In my room.'

'How did it get there?'

'I don't know.'

'Had he arranged to meet you there?'

'He had arranged to come and give me a paper.'

I noticed that the two sisters were then looking at Alex with a sudden new interest, but neither spoke.

'Were you there when he came?' I said.

'No. I came and found him. I didn't know exactly what time he meant to come.'

'So you didn't get the paper?'

'No. I'll be honest, I searched for it, but it wasn't on him.'

'He was dead then?'

'Quite dead. I looked but couldn't find any wound or any marks as if he'd been struck except on his forehead, and there was a plaster on that.'

'Then what happened?'

'I went and told Ralph.' Alex looked at her brother. 'He came back with me and had a look. He went into a bit of a tizz for a minute or two, and then he said it had better be got rid of.'

I looked at Ralph.

'Why did you suggest that?' I said.

He sat back in his chair and looked at me.

'Why?' he said. 'Mr. Gaunt, there is a very good reason why I don't know why I should have suggested anything. I never heard this rigmarole before.'

'Ralph — you liar!' Alex cried.

'Me? That's rich! You suddenly spring a load of hay on me and then say I'm a liar for not knowing what in hell you're talking about. What's the idea, Alex?'

Her sisters were watching her with keen interest and I felt sure they hadn't heard this story before, either.

'Very well!' said Alex, and with all of Mama's inherited drama, she got up and walked off and out of the room.

'Did she call you?' Georgie said, turning to Ralph.

'What sort of paper would he have

given her?' Ralph said. 'What sort of paper that was so important? Does it make any sense?'

I watched them while thinking of the whole thing. If Ralph had asked me in just to clear him from any dirt, then what he was doing fitted very well.

If he really wanted to know what had happened to his short-lost uncle, then I was being unkind to him, but I felt he wanted to know only for his own comfort.

There was no way of taking Alex's story of the body in the bedroom and the promised paper. I bore in mind that so far they had been a group of entertaining liars with more care for the amusing side than for the truth or of any details.

The picture they had drawn of Mama bore no resemblance to the woman I had met, and though they had played it quiet at dinner there had been no evidence of any browbeating by Mama.

And certainly no evidence that the daughters would do as they were told at any time. The main purpose of the members of the Van Deken family seemed to be to disagree with each other over everything.

'Is the story of the body in her bedroom true?' I said.

'No,' said Charlie. 'It was on the landing when I saw it. That's why it had to be moved. Dudley did it.'

'He put it in the airing cupboard,' Georgie said. 'That's where I saw it.'

'That's right,' said Ralph. 'I helped Dudley down into the woods with it — ' He broke off and bashed the table with his fist. 'What's the good of telling these lies? You know where it was! Charlotte, Georgina — you saw it in the bushes down by the river. You both saw it there and so did I.'

I sat back.

'I'm tired of this,' I said. 'I can't make head or tail of what you are trying to do. You should have agreed a story between the lot of you beforehand. All you're doing now is tying each other up in knots.

'The result is, I don't believe he's dead. What you called me down for, lord knows. There must be a strong reason, but I can't think of any logical one.

'In the circumstances, I have decided to regard the whole thing as an infantile hoax, and thank you for the entertainment. Goodbye.'

I got up and walked out to the hall. All three followed me to the door, the ladies asking me pretty fiercely not to go. Ralph said nothing.

He came out with me into the hall and closed the door on his sisters.

In the hall he looked round for my coat and saw it on the floor in the corner.

'I'm sorry about it,' he said quietly, and gave me the coat. 'The game you have just witnessed was trying to find out who really knew where it was. We all know he's here, but we can't find out where.'

'I don't believe any of it — '

'Please. I am sure he's in the Treasure Room on the top floor. That's why Alex started on about hearing somebody up there banging on her ceiling. It's part of the same game of trying to make somebody say pooh too hard. We are experts in judging each other's tones of voice.'

'I will give you your cheque — '

'I don't want it. I asked you to do this for me. If there is no murder when you get to the bottom of it, so much the better. But I must know, either way.

'I know my family is very trying, and I agree with your going now, but I would be most grateful if you'd do as I first asked you — to come back tonight and look into the Treasure Room. It is that which I want most of all.'

I thought a moment. I admitted to myself that I wanted to know what all this tangled nonsense was about, because I did not believe that this lot of self-centred sophisticates were inventing lies without some idea of personal gain in the background.

That had to be the reason why every personal story disagreed with the next.

'I'll do that,' I said at last, 'but if I draw a blank, you have your cheque and I go back to my office. There is one thing I want the truth about before I leave now.'

He hesitated a second or two.

'What is that?'

'Had Clarence money?'

'I believe he had. I don't know for certain, but I believe he had money in Australia. He had come on a visit to see Mama and the girls mainly. A sentimental journey.'

'But he had only a small case.'

'That's true.'

He opened the main door for me.

'I'll leave this unlocked,' he said, and held out his closed hand. 'This is one key to the room. I can't get the duplicate of the second key. They have to be used together. Can you manage?'

'I shall have to see when the time comes.'

I drove to the main gates which opened at my approach and closed behind me as I turned out into the street. I had no doubt Ralph had switched the mechanism on for me, as if left to do it whenever approached why have gates at all?

★ ★ ★

At the pub I got to my room without meeting anybody. The promised sandwiches were there, and I was hungry by then.

Lying on the bed afterwards and thinking of the evening and the Victorian half dresses the scene seemed less charming and sharply amusing as it had been then.

In memory, and away from the atmosphere of the house, it had the queer colours of Grand Guignol. As if the half naked chorus were a prelude to the raising of the curtain upon a scene of blood and carnage.

Lying there I felt they knew what had happened; they knew where Clarence was, and they had done it for the money they pretend he hadn't had.

If that were so it would be necessary to find out if the Van Deken millions still existed, although if they did that would clear only Mama.

The daughters and sons were waiting for money. Were spending their lives idly waiting for it. The sudden appearance of a rich Uncle with no relatives but themselves might have proved enchanting.

I slept for two hours and woke at one thirty. I left the pub by the car-park door and went over the back wall into the house grounds; the way Clarence had come on his last visit to Annie.

Carefully working my way through the gardens I needed my torch, for the town lights had then gone out.

The feeling I had as I got nearer the house was that I was going to find Clarence. Why I felt it for sure, I didn't know, unless it had been Ralph's insistence from the first that I go and look.

At that time it never crossed my mind that this visit might be a very long one; that I might never get out of the house at all.

That would have been too dramatic, and I am not a dramatic person. At least, I wasn't at that time.

As promised, the house door opened when the handle was turned. There was a very faint sort of night lighting in the hall, just enough to see by.

Unfortunately, also just enough to be

seen by, should anyone wake.

It was quiet when I stepped into the hall and closed the door. Mama's story of her children being dependable watchdogs did not seem to have much truth in it.

As Ralph had mentioned somewhere, everyone slept on the first floor, so that once I had passed that level and gone on up to the top, the risk of waking someone should be less.

I went up the stairs. The Van Deken carpets were as deep as the family's dishonesty. There was no sound of my footfalls.

When I reached the first floor landing I heard no noise of anybody awake and went on up to the top floor.

The same very subdued light was glowing on each landing, and I thought that perhaps Ralph had left the lights on for my benefit.

There was no problem about finding the door of the Treasure Room, for it was the only one which had two locks. I had a close look at the keyholes with my torch and decided that the top one would be difficult to pick and might take some time.

The key I had been given turned the bottom lock easily so I brought out a small wallet of instruments and selected two for an attack on the top one.

Probing it made me think that perhaps it was not quite as difficult as it looked, but all the same it must have taken me almost ten minutes before I had the thing in my control and clicked it open.

Both locks free, I tried the handle, but as I did so there was a woman's shout from somewhere below.

'Somebody's upstairs! On the top landing! Ralph! Dudley!'

There was only one thing for me to do then, and that was to open the secret door, step in, take out the key and pick, and close it again.

I closed it. There was no light inside the room. It was dark and there was a smell I could not place for a moment or two.

Death. It smelt of death. Beyond the door the sudden alarm sounded like something worse.

# 7

I kept quite still in the darkness of the room, listening to the growing commotion of alarm on the other side. The women were mostly in evidence by their cries and shouts of disagreement as to what ought to be done.

Then I heard Ralph's voice.

'Oh, stop it!' he commanded, very loudly. 'We don't even know there is anybody in the house. It's only Fanny's word and she's on edge!'

Fanny immediately repudiated the suggestion of her being near any edge, and an argument, cleverly stoked by Ralph, took fire amongst the ladies and they waded in with full noisy vigour. Even Mama, apparently bellowing from the landing below, had no effect on the clamour.

I could not get out and I would not use any light in case it showed under the door, so I thought it well to view the scene while they argued and prevented me getting on with my job.

Being where I was I suppose my thoughts were turned by the wish to be in my bed at the pub.

Therefore I thought of the conversations I had had there, especially about the reputation of the house and Mama.

Two things came into my mind then, because I didn't like the smell of the room I was in, I suppose.

One was the suggestion that a man had called and tried to interest Mama in ghosts. The story presumed he was never seen again.

There was also another suggestion about men who had called on Mama and had never come out.

Somehow that connected with Dudley's remark that Mama had seemed alarmed when Clarence turned up.

According to the confused lies and tales of the family, Clarence had been away for as long as Van Deken had been dead, roughly. And Mama had been alarmed when he turned up.

Had I, while trying to soothe my mind

against possible capture, struck a motive for murder at last?

The argument outside, about what they should do to trap the burglar conducted in a cross fire of bawls that there was no burglar, and another sniping of whose nerves were on the blink and the ack-ack of Mama shouting orders from below suddenly came to an end.

There was silence.

Silence made me uneasy, as if they had decided something and that to pursue the burglar, whether he was there or not.

Ralph took volume control.

'SHUT UP AND GO BACK TO BED!'

The offensive immediately turned against him, and the clamour began to go downstairs, apparently in pursuit of Ralph.

How on earth they all put up with each other was a bigger mystery to me than the rest of the business.

I began to feel relieved as the noise died down, but then Mama's voice overcame everything else.

'What are you doing? Get up there

and find the burglar!'

I recognised Alex saying. 'Why don't you go yourself? You can get up anything and over everybody!'

'Out of my way!' cried Mama. 'If you're all too frightened, let me go! And don't follow me! I forbid you!'

The voices died away. I listened at the door intently. I heard Mama's footfalls as she resolutely mounted the stairs.

She knew I was in her secret room. I felt sure of it.

I heard her come close to the door and turn the handle. My nerves were then quite stiff.

The fact she turned the handle indicated she thought the door was unlocked.

In fact it wasn't, but her next step was to think it had been relocked once I was inside.

There was a hiss.

'Can you hear me, my dear?' she whispered through one of the keyholes.

I kept dead still.

The whisper was startling, driving in to my head questions different from the one she asked.

Was Clarence dead after all? Was it a put-up job to bamboozle her family?

The second, perhaps, indicated a concerted deception.

Had Clarence come back to the Van Dekens at all?

But the second question seemed to be answered by the fact that both Annie and Mary had met him on very close terms.

But was the man they knew Clarence, or a stand-in procured for the deception? I heard Mama breathing rather fast on the other side of the door. I thought it indicated rising anger.

She whispered again more sharply.

'Sweetie! Open the door!'

There was nothing else to do but lie doggo and breathe very carefully, hoping I wouldn't sneeze.

I heard Mama say something very vulgar, perhaps supposing no one could hear it, then she seemed to turn and, from the sounds, went to the stairs and started down.

I heard the family begin to call to her, asking if anybody was up there.

'Nobody is up there,' she said, regally.

She sounded so dignified I thought of the incredible bare back view in magnificent retreat. 'There is nothing wrong in this house tonight but your trembling nerves. Now get back to your rooms and shiver in silence!'

Gradually silence took over.

I breathed slow and deep for a half minute to ease the nervous tension on my muscles. Why the family should have such a frightening effect on the senses was a mystery to me.

Outwardly charming, amusing, eccentric and wayward morally, yet somehow there was a chill core that after a while of association with them, began to radiate fear.

I waited until I was quite sure no one was outside, then turned on my light. Anticipation of some horror coloured my first sight of this musty museum as the torch beam picked out shot by shot.

Grotesque African masks, witch doctors' get ups, spears, warriors' shields, beads, tribal ornaments, all hanging like stalactites from the ceiling beams, a sort of dusty curtain left by dead fear-makers.

There were even shrunken heads hanging by their long hair in clusters like wizened fruit.

If this display of fantasy from past travels repeated Mama's care for her lost husband, then her memory of him was dusty indeed.

As I moved forward down the long room, the dust began to tickle my nostrils, like at hay-making in early summer.

The way through — the avenue, as it were, was crooked and twisting and the path was continually pushed into another shape by heaps of mementoes just piled in and left, or hung up in strings, growing cobwebs.

I stopped and looked back when half-way along, because the ragbag of stuff was not all from travels. There were a couple of garish-faced rocking horses crammed in amongst the rubbish, and several child's dolls were dropped around anywhere.

Why on earth have an expensive double lock put on to protect such a heap of dusty muck was a question for a lunatic. He might see the reason. I couldn't.

It had smelt of death, but it was the death even of memories of death.

Looking back at the door and wondering what it was all for, the torchbeam edged the floor I'd walked along.

I had made no footprints because there was no dust on the boards.

Most other things seemed to have plenty of dust and cobwebs above, but the crooked path between the rubbish was clear of it.

So Mama did come here.

I shone the torch up amongst the stalactites of beads, thongs, ropes, and native chains of stripwood but saw no light fitting.

Perhaps, like Lady Macbeth, she used a candle when she came.

But why did she come?

Turning my back to the door again I followed the crazy path round to one side, then to the other until, looking back, I could not see the door for the festoons of memories hanging from the roof beams.

Going on again very slowly in case there should be something which could enlighten in this clutter, I came near the right hand wall and there was an oddity.

A white porcelain sink with chrome hot and cold taps was fixed to the wall. The gleaming whiteness and the shining silver taps in that cavern of webs made an astonishing sight.

I remembered Alex in the dining room saying she had heard somebody knocking, and the brother's assurance that it was the water knocking as usual.

The inside of the sink was not clean, as a lot of the dust from above had drifted down and streaked the bottom. The little channels in the dust on the sink bottom were damp when I put a finger to test.

I turned and looked behind me. The piles of boxes and unsorted stuff was like a cliff, but to the right of it, the great room went on even deeper into the dark.

It was not in fact a room, but an attic running out over a whole wing of the house.

As I turned to look down the further reaches of the place I heard the door rattle faintly, as if the draperies of beads and cobwebs muffled the real sound.

I turned off the light and stood quite still, listening.

There was no heated whispering this time, but a pause and then the door rattled again, the second time more violently than before.

A few seconds passed with no sound at all, and then I heard a slight scratching sound which hardly travelled the distance to where I was.

The sound was puzzling and it continued intermittently for more than a minute before I realised what was going on.

Someone was picking the locks.

★ ★ ★

It was difficult to imagine who would be doing that. Certainly not Mama, she had retreated believing she had made an error in thinking someone was inside.

Secondly she wouldn't have come back and then tried the door handle. She had done that already and found the locks shot. She would have come back and started picking straight away — if she hadn't found her keys.

But it was a good double lock to pick, though I say it myself, having picked half of it, and forcing the two together would present problems.

Even as I thought that, I heard one lock click with the firm sound of the bolt shifting back.

I shielded the head of my torch with my hand and switched on again. With that restricted light I moved further back into the depths of the attic.

I came near a low, long table, which had what looked in that distorted light like an unfinished mummy lying on it. I stopped and started to uncover the light when there was a crash from back at the door.

I couldn't tell what it was but it sounded like the door giving way under pressure, and I turned out the light and again stood still.

There was no sound after the crash. I peered in the direction of the door but no light shone between the weeds of rubbish hanging from the ceiling.

The landing light had been on and if the door opened it should have showed through because of the intensity of the dark in the attic, but I saw nothing.

Perhaps it had not been the door being forced that I'd heard, but some other way in which had no light behind it.

There was no sound anywhere for several seconds and then came a small, soft noise. The strain of listening was so great I did not recognise the dripping of water into the sink for two or three seconds.

There was only a solitary drop, but neither tap had been dripping when I had seen them not more than a minute before.

Something must have disturbed the sink very slightly and shaken out a drop that had been held up the curved nozzle.

An entrance near the sink, not the far-off door at all. With all the sound blanketing of the hangings and heaps of stuff lying around, any sound heard was bound to be deceptive from damping.

Someone had come into that attic, but

was standing as still and listening as hard as I was.

I could not guess which of the household the intruder might be, but he or she was guilty, and suddenly I believed I was standing by the secret of that guilt.

The unfinished Mummy.

Windings of the dead, half done. A sink provided for the washing away of difficult matter like blood.

A dead man after all. A dead man on the table right by me.

It was logical that if the intruder found me, he would have to kill me as well.

I was standing over his secret.

And perhaps not the only one. Mummy winding might be a hobby for him. The story of men going into that house and not being seen again might have truth in it.

My imagination was going strong in the dark, knowing a murderer was somewhere near and listening for me to make a sound.

I have had practice at keeping still in awkward situations but it is always a nervous strain that needs a lot of relief when the tension ends.

There was a soft thump. A second later, a tap dripped again, twice.

I let a minute or more go by, straining myself to keep up the stillness, though I had the idea the thump had been the closing of the secret door.

Hearing nothing and seeing no light in the gloomy place, the intruder might have supposed no one was there after all.

I relaxed slowly, breathing very quietly, but gratefully, even in that close atmosphere.

At first I held my hand tightly over the torch head when I switched on, but after a few seconds freed the light.

The mummy was almost fully bound but for the feet. There were all kinds of pots and jars of stuff which probably helped the obscene work on its way.

Someone must have found it an entertaining hobby, for carrying it out must take a great deal of one's spare time, not to mention the cost in nervous energy.

I turned the light away from the body

and down the rest of the attic. More stuff, piled up anywhere, with twisted little paths left between, as before, but in amongst the stuff I saw mummy cases.

There were three parked around in different parts of the mess.

I left the table and went down a twisted path to the nearest. The great painted face, staring slightlessly into the top of my head unnerved me for a second.

It was standing with its sides fairly clear of clutter, but I did not know how to burgle a mummy. I was not really anxious to look inside it; my fastidious nature was against seeing something rotten.

All I knew was that the lid came off somehow. I tapped on the case, but it was very solid. I rocked it slightly, but it took so much effort I couldn't tell if it had any tenant or not.

I went back to the table.

The feet were clean, pale, like wax and looked cared for, though I am no judge of feet.

I wished I could see the face under the wrappings, but did nothing to get a look, telling myself that I did not know

Clarence's looks anyhow.

There were mummy cases, and there was this body, so there was murder.

Murder was certain in my mind because no one would go to any length to hide a normally dead person.

And there had been so much talk about the subject of murder that it had got into my mind.

Now I had made certain of it, there was murder, I felt unkeen to get too near it. I have had experience of such things, but in the vicarious manner of finding out what happened and then letting the ogres go in and contact the factual evidence.

Unfortunate sudden shocks of the fleshly sort can upset the digestion for days, and the palate goes sour.

Up to that time, I suppose I had enjoyed the Van Dekens, but I had believed that the continued barrage of murder suggestions was a part of their morbid fancy.

At the back of my mind I suppose I had thought the Clarence affair as a murder case to have been a cover for something else, much more profitable.

Now that I had penetrated the secret room, it appeared that there was no real gain but in the finding and revealing of murder, and there is no profit in that.

The original idea of calling me because Clarence had asked Ralph to do so was good, if Clarence had been the sort to wish for revenge after death.

From what I had heard of him he wouldn't have given a damn what happened to him after death.

Once more I looked at the pale, bare feet and the idea of starting to undo the bandages stirred in my mind, but again I argued, what good would it do?

I couldn't identify any body likely to be in this place.

The important thing for me then was to begin a search amongst the mass of forgotten stuff for a sign of a recent or regular disturbance.

There was too much of it to be meticulous, but I picked certain areas which I could see from standing by the mummy table, and searched those.

There was no sign of anything having

been looked at closely for years.

A further search, by walking down the path to the door scanning one side with the light beam, then the other when coming back, still showed no sign of recent attention.

At that point I began to think the treasure room had been used merely to lure people into for the purpose of murder.

A sort of fairy tale trap: 'Look into the sink, dear, it grants wishes,' and the victim looks and — clunk! — off comes his head.

That way of looking at it suited Mama, perhaps and it might have been partly true.

But why?

I had met Mama. I had watched Mama. I had watched her mannerisms, her eyes and other details whereby one can detect the abnormal, the wayward, the barmy.

She had appeared as rational as any millionaire intent on keeping his lot from the baying mob.

Leaning my backside against the sink,

I turned out the light and thought very hard about the whole story as it had happened to me, and it led me back to the puzzle at the beginning.

The inexplicably large offer of a thousand pounds a week to find out something that could not materially benefit Ralph.

Clarence had suggested it, and me as his finder. That much had to be certain, for I had never been near this place before and not heard of the Van Deken family until Ralph had made them audible to me.

The answer to the mystery of how and why Clarence did know of me was surely that we had known each other when he had used another name.

What else could it have been but that?

I don't advertise my detective work. I am part of a firm which makes no publicity of its enquiry side.

Yet Ralph van Deken knew and called me, and as I didn't know him, I now felt sure Clarence must have known me.

But why would Clarence, carefree

libertine and free liver, want his fate found out anyway?

And why should Ralph pay for this service?

There was a trap somewhere in this whole arrangement; a trap I could fall into, but I could not see where it was, what form it took, or why it should be set at all.

I leaned off the sink and shone the light up and down the alleys of the attic, just in case some glaring oversight should show itself, but it didn't.

The tap dripped once behind me. I turned and shone the light on the fixing of the sink against the wooden wall.

At that point the wall was lined with matchboarding fixed in vertical strips.

I could see no horizontal cuts indicating an opening in the wallboarding and turned the light to the floor.

As elsewhere, the floor was fairly clean and I looked around for a trapdoor for a while before I realised it was a waste of time.

The man on the table had been murdered, I fairly assumed, and probably he had been invited in. If he had been killed outside the attic, then he had been carried or dragged in.

Neither of these entrances would have been effected through a small trapdoor.

Entrance must have been made through the one door with the double lock.

There might be some sort of spyhole through the boarding behind the sink, but I could find nothing of it.

My visit to the treasure room was proving to be a flop.

There was a corpse and maybe others, but the reasons for it all, the thing I had come to find, just did not show itself.

I thought then that it could not be in the attic at all, and went back to the double-locked door.

# 8

The picking needed light and I laid my torch on a pile of boxes nearby so the beam shone on the door, and then set about opening the locks.

The click of victory came from the second lock as I heard a voice in the corridor outside.

It was most unfortunate, for should anyone try the door, they would find it unlocked and find me as well.

I stood very still and listened.

Mama's voice sounded clearly.

'Fanny! Open your door. I want to come in!'

It seemed that Fanny answered from inside her room but I couldn't hear what she said.

'I have hurt my arm and need attention,' said Mama, very loudly.

I risked opening the door a fraction and peered out along the passage. Mama was standing talking to the door of a room down the passage.

'I am also scared stiff by myself because of this burglar and as you're the only one I can trust I will come in with you.'

Again Fanny mumbled something.

Whatever she said did not meet with Mama's approval.

She smashed on the door with her fists.

'Open this bloody door, Fatima!' she said furiously.

I heard bolts and chains being undone and then the door came open.

Mama strode in as if to tread any opposition underfoot. The door shut behind her. The corridor became quiet again, and I could hear nothing in the house at all.

Once out in the passage I closed the door but did not relock it. I went halfway down the stairs and then looked over the rails to the landing below and directly down into hall.

There was no sign of anyone moving below and I went on down very quietly.

The door directly opposite the foot of

the stairs was ajar, as if someone had left that room in a hurry. I assumed it was Mama's room, since she had been agitated in her demand to get into Fanny's room upstairs.

It was clear there were no special locks on the half open door, as it was usually enough, perhaps to fear Mama's presence inside to deter the inquisitive.

As I reached the landing I looked carefully up and down the corridor, then crossed the thick carpet, went into the room and closed the door behind me. I also turned the key.

The room led into another. The whole arrangement was a suite, a flat with all conveniences, where one could stay and sulk for days without discomfort.

It was pretty rich with gold, satin, lace, Chinese carpets and other simple devices beloved of part-time hermits.

I went through into the bedroom and looked round for a suitable situation for a safe.

There were several, like pictures, mantlepieces, the backs of cupboards and so forth, and of such hiding places the least obvious is the obvious place to look first.

In Mama's case I was not so sure. She was an opulent extrovert and probably told everybody she'd got a safe so it was quite likely to be on show, probably with a laugh-surprise to it.

And thus, when I saw an ornate Georgian commode in the bedchamber, I decided to start there. In fact, I had no further to go.

With the lid up the interior looked authentic, but by experimenting with the seat I made it click by pushing backwards, and the porcelain utensils slid to one side and below smiled the face of the safe.

As I searched, I had listened intently for any sign of activity, and heard nothing. A family of sound sleepers despite Mama's assurance to the contrary.

With my small tools I have a telescopic listening rod with an earpiece, which contains a Japanese amplifier which makes the simple type of combination lock less effective.

It is not a refined instrument, as the

lock sounds like a tube train thundering through a tunnel until tumblers fall with crashes like volcanic explosions in the sensitive ear, but there is no fine control, so the operator has to suffer in the cause of possible future benefit.

The forcing of the lock took just over seven minutes, including pauses to listen for intruders.

An important moment in the art of safebreaking is when the lock is free and the act of opening the door might set off an alarm.

My precaution against this had been to move the commode across the floor to make sure no wires were about, but to make quite certain I searched again and found nothing.

The safe door opened like the breech of a gun, and there was quite a lot of room inside the steel cell. More than there should have been, for the safe was empty.

The emptiness of the safe revived the brief but funny idea I had had not long before: that Clarence had money and Mama had not.

What that situation gave was an offbeat motive, provided that Clarence had no relatives of his own sowing, and judging from his recent history, that was, mathematically, unlikely.

The next thing was to look around for a second storage place for anything of value. It was then I realised that I had not looked in the most likely place, but in the most likely humorous place.

I went to the dressing table, the top an untidy mess of enamel backed silver brushes and other tools, open powders, puffs lying about, a string of pearls, eye-brow tweezers, lipsticks and bottles of all shapes and decorative sizes.

It looked like Mama's favourite muck-heap, where she could sit for hours looking at herself and testing out paints, even in stripes down her face if she felt like it.

When I opened a drawer in the dressing table it was a mess of pots, papers, lipsticks and banknotes. Hundreds of banknotes all mixed around with false eyelashes and cornplasters.

In the companion drawer on the

other side there were necklaces, earrings, bracelets, rings, diamond belts, coat clips, brooches and some pieces of which I had no idea where they could have been worn.

It was difficult to know which pieces to choose when such a lot was suddenly presented under one's nose.

But there were no documents or deeds. Such a possessive person as Mama with her built-in certainty that all men were fools, I felt sure would keep such papers to herself rather than park them out in a bank or with solicitors.

And there were none at all. Not even an insurance policy over which she had said she argued once a year.

The lack made me take a careful look in the room, into cupboards and drawers and anywhere else experience told me people kept papers, but found none.

Nobody, it seemed, wrote to Mama. There were no letters. I thought that very odd and I went on to make sure I'd missed no hiding place.

While doing that I had made up my

mind and went back to the drawer and took out some pieces which were of the highest value and most convenient size. I folded them in a clean handkerchief and put the packet into my breast pocket.

That done I pulled out the drawers and tossed them, upside down on the bed. After that I pulled out other drawers, dropped two on the bed, leaned three up against the wall as if they had landed after being thrown, left others in place and went to the door.

The same silence was on in the place. I unlocked the door, opened it and listened again. Nothing.

I rushed out and shouted 'Stop!'

That done I ran downstairs to the hall as fast as I could, calling out twice. I reached the front door and opened it fast, looking behind me up the stairs as I did.

'Here!' I bawled and ran out into the night.

Silence rewarded me out there. Behind me I heard sounds of the alarm being raised.

With considerable courage and devotion

to stern principles, I punched myself hard on the nose and then staggered back into the hall fumbling a handkerchief out of my pocket.

'What is it!' Mama's strident shout came clearly to me even above the pain in my nose.

Ralph came rushing down the stairs with Charlie right behind him and the other two daughters calling down from the landing rail.

'What's happened?' Ralph shouted.

'A burglar!' I said. My nose was bleeding a lot and I began to fear I had overdone things.

'Oh, you've been hit!' said Charlie coming forward. 'Oh, poor man. You come with me. I'll fix it for you. Come on.'

She grabbed my arm and dragged me into a cloak room by the side of the hall. There she got a wet flannel and smacked it on my nose.

'Blow,' she said.

The others were crowding in behind us, all asking questions.

'How can he answer?' said Georgie

impatiently. 'She's holding his bloody nose!'

Charlie made me sit in a chair, despite my protests and made me tip my head back and so on.

When the bleeding stopped and I let my head go back to normal the family parted like the Red Sea and Mama came through.

'I have been robbed!' she said. 'You saw him!'

'Only for a moment,' I said, drying my face on the towel Charlie provided.

'How did you come to be here?' said Mama, slowly.

'I couldn't sleep. I thought I would look in your wood for some sign of Clarence, but when I started I saw your front door open. It was late. I was naturally curious.'

Mama looked round at her brood.

'He must have been in the house for hours,' she said. 'I told you, but nobody would listen!'

'You said there wasn't anybody up there,' said Alex. 'So cut out the I-told-you-so bit.'

They argued for a while. As I had betted with myself, nobody suggested calling the police.

'What about that junk butler?' said Georgie from the back.

'He went hours ago,' said Ralph.

I noticed Fanny standing at the back of the crowd, watching.

It was Alex who put in the poison.

'Where's Dudley?' she said loudly. 'Is he dead or something?'

The rest kept properly quiet to underline the fact that despite all the alarm and hullaballoo, Dudley hadn't joined the desperate band of burglar raisers.

* * *

'Go and knock him up,' said Ralph.

It was Alex who went. She was frowning as if she did not quite agree with the general attitude of attack on Dudley.

In that family, none agreed with another except when they were considering Dudley, then they closed ranks. I felt a little sorry for him.

I got up.

'What have you lost, Mrs. Van Deken?'

'I don't know,' she said.

'But you just said you'd been robbed.'

'Yes, I've been robbed but I don't know what's gone.'

The children were watching and listening with special care, as if the missing stuff belonged to them already.

'Surely you have some idea — ?'

'I have a great deal of jewellery, Mr. Gaunt, and there is no list, no inventory. But on looking in my drawer I see there is a less of a heap than there was before.'

'I don't quite understand. Do you mean there is a lot of valuable jewellery there still? In the drawer with the stolen pieces?'

'That is what I mean. Yes.'

'And you go by the size of the heap to show whether anything is missing?'

'With my family, I am expert in judging the size of heaps, Mr. Gaunt.'

Georgie breathed hissingly through her nose. Ralph laughed. Charlie clicked with her tongue in disapproval.

'Would you like me to look at the room?'

'No, I would not like you to look at the room.'

'Well, I can hardly help you, can I? Clearly, I interrupted the man's escape, but not enough.'

'Your nose looks terrible,' said Mama.

My heart quailed as the thought I might have broken my nose crossed my mind. I felt it, but though swollen, the bone and gristle seemed as sound as before and I was relieved.

'You said somebody was upstairs,' said Georgie, who hadn't even put a dressing gown over her musical pyjamas. 'Mama. You said somebody was upstairs and told us to go to bed after you'd been up there.'

Fanny was up there. I asked her if anybody had been upstairs. She said no.'

'When Fanny gets nervous she blocks her ears up,' said Charlie, who apparently went to bed in her several necklaces. 'She wouldn't hear anybody.'

I was trying not to ask Mama why she

had whispered through the keyhole, and it was difficult to hold back.

To whom had she thought she'd whispered? Why would anyone have been waiting in the Treasure Room, where the dead man was?

The embalmer? Would she call a midnight mortician Sweetie? Even granting Mama might do anything, it seemed unlikely.

Then was it Clarence up there? Was it Clarence who came in through a trap by the sink? In the course of his extensive travels and odd trades had he come across the art of making mummies of dead bodies?

Did she suspect Clarence of having rifled her drawer and that was the reason no police had been mentioned?

Fanny interrupted my thoughts.

'Don't you think you ought to lie down, madam?' she said, taking Mama's arm. 'You have had a shock, you know. Come along, I'll make you comfortable.'

Mama's fury slowly faded.

'Thank you, Fanny. Most thoughtful. Most thoughtful.'

And with that meek note, she let herself be led away. If nothing else, Mama was a first class ham. No bad actor would have been so bad so well as she.

I looked at the two daughters and Ralph, who was watching Mama being led up the stairs.

'Let's get out of the bog, to start with,' said Georgie inelegantly. 'Then we can talk this over.'

'I was thinking,' I said, 'shouldn't you call the police?'

'Oh no,' she said. 'Mama hates strangers poking around amongst her things.'

'Besides, she doesn't know if she's lost anything, and that insurance man will try and bully her about it because she wouldn't increase the risk,' said Charley. 'So probably she wouldn't get anything if she did claim.'

'Well, if she's willing to bear the loss — ' I said.

'I'll pay for your face,' said Ralph. 'Don't worry about that'.

'How much are noses?' said Georgie.

165

We went into the hall.

I felt physically good, despite my nose. Everything was working out for the best — my best, that is to say. I had judged the family well, and that surely was worth a fee?

I felt that with a win under my belt I should be sitting down to a glorious supper of roast duckling and orange sauce, preceded by a dozen oysters, and all helped along by a bottle of the Widow's champagne of any year; I would not be fussy about that. Then watercress and Stilton —

I was very hungry. I think perhaps excitement causes it sometimes.

'You say the butler left?' I said.

'We kicked him forth,' said Ralph. 'I wonder now whether he could have had something to do with the burglary.'

He looked at me.

'But you paid him for his hurt?' I said.

'It was an accident,' said George. 'He fell over backwards and bashed his head on a rolling pin on the table.'

'Oh,' I said, marvelling, 'yes. I suppose

he could have done that very easily.'

'I gave him a fiver tip for the bash,' said Ralph.

Pushing the thought of a meal out of my mind, my euphoria unable to support the dream. It was evaporating under a need to consider my situation.

With presence of mind, or unwillingness to lose anything of mine, perhaps, I had kept strong hold on my torch, which assisted the story of walking in the woods.

But there was the question of why I hadn't shone it at the burglar's face. No one had asked it, but I was sure someone would.

It was a minor thing, but so is a trip-cord. I worked it out that as I had started to chase, running, of course, the man had turned suddenly and belted me in the nose.

There was also a matter of more importance. Somebody knew I had been by the death table in the treasure room.

They might not have known it was me, but elimination is a simple process.

There was a developing problem coming from that person, which was going to ask why I had found a dead body in an unauthorised place and not reported it to authority outside.

In that problem I had to depend on the person not wishing me to do such a thing, because if I did, he would be chopped.

'What's happened to Alex?' Charlie said.

'She's looking for dear Duds,' said Georgie. 'Don't you remember?'

'Dear Duds takes some waking once he's off, what with grass and similar aids to dreams,' said Ralph.

I looked from one to the other of them because for a moment, they were all looking at me.

'Who did thump the butler?' I said, then raised a hand. 'Don't think I'm criticising. If any butler deserved it — and so on. But who?'

'The fact is,' said Ralph, 'and this is the truth, believe me, nobody knows who did it.'

'Nobody of us,' corrected Georgie.

'Nobody of us,' Ralph agreed.

'Only Fanny was left, or Alex,' I said.

'Neither would boff somebody's head, however thick,' said Ralph. 'Besides — why? What mileage do we get from thudding a hired chump?'

'He was outstanding,' I said. 'I'm certain he was never a chauffeur either. He knew nothing of service. He was a thick insult.'

'Clarence recommended,' said Georgie.

'Clarence was a comedian,' said Charlie, shortly.

I thought I would make as much of the mysterious bogus butler as possible.

'Are you sure an agency sent him?' I said.

'No doubt of that,' Ralph said. 'But I should think they mistook butler for cutler or some such. But yes. We pay the account to them, so it has to be right.'

'I'm going to get a sandwich,' Charlie said. 'I'm starving and it's getting chilly out here.'

'Let's get some for all three — four,' said Georgie and went with her.

Ralph waited until they'd gone.

'What did you find up there?' he said anxiously.

'When did you last go in there?'

'I nicked her keys once, but she got wind of it and almost as soon as I got in, she came up outside.'

'But when?'

'Just before Clarence came. A week back.'

'Why did you go?'

'It's one of those things. Bluebeard's locked room. You know the temptation.'

'But what did you find in there?'

'Surely you know? You saw it!'

'I saw a lot of rubbish. Old things brought back from travels. What did you see?'

'Well, the same.'

'Mummies?'

'Oh, there's two or three of those, but I think they're just the cases. Nothing in them. The departed spirits were sold off, I expect.'

'You saw the sink?'

'Yes.'

'And the low table opposite?'

'Yes.'

'Well, what was on the table?'

He stared at me, and for the first time

I thought he might be genuinely puzzled and not just faking innocence.

'Pots and brushes. Things like that,' he said.

'And that's all?'

'That's all I saw. But there's such a welter of muck in there I was a bit confused by it all. Lord knows why she keeps it all. And locked up! It can't be valuable. I mean — '

Alex came quickly down the stairs. She looked calm, but pale and very determined.

She came up to us.

'Dudley is dead,' she said. 'He's been murdered.'

# 9

The sisters and brother looked at each other in a sort of dumb shock, then looked at me as if I could help in the predicament.

At that time I wasn't interested in helping them. If Dudley had been murdered then I was in a sore predicament myself.

There having been no burglar but me, and no known intruder but me, then anybody dying from malicious causes would be blamed on me.

Ralph had let me in and probably knew there hadn't been anyone else wandering around the place that night. In any case, once serious trouble had occurred he was bound to say he had let me in and my story of being in the woods would be revealed as a lie.

It would then quickly be surmised that no burglar had been in the place that night. Only me.

Mama had noticed a slight difference in the shape of her heap of jewels, and those I had considered superfluous to her needs or comfort were in my pocket and would now be difficult to get rid of before somebody suspected.

The way out for me in law, of course, was to say I had found a dead body, if not more, in the attic, and that would give rise to the idea that the murderer had merely added Dudley to his collection.

Such things mashed round in my mind in heavy indecision caused by a depression founded on the idea that whatever I did to get on the right side of legal processes, I had had it.

My time had run out, and the time I was likely to get in extension would be at the disposal of the judge.

'You'd better look at it, Mr. Gaunt,' said Alex.

'If you wish,' I said.

The very sound of that bogus name sent an added shiver through my guilty soul. Though Ralph knew it was false he did not know that the name he thought was real was also false.

I went ahead with Alex up the stairs with the others following. At the top she turned left and opened a door on the left again of the corridor.

It was what is generally known as a bed-sitter of a room, overloaded with musical instruments, books, magazines and half finished paintings showing little talent.

Dudley was lying back on an old chaise longue, staring at the ceiling. He was in shirt and trousers and I did not see any signs of wounds, so I went to the raised end of the settee and looked at him from there.

There was some disturbance at the back of his head. I had a closer look, swallowed my disgust that I should have to submit to such horrors for the sake of saving myself.

'He's been struck from behind,' I said, backing off quickly. 'Like the butler.'

With some relief I turned away from the corpse and began to look around for some likely weapon.

An innate, though partly disused, honesty of purpose took command, and

174

I began to think less of myself, and more of why dreamy, rather stupid, Dudley should have been slammed out of this world while enjoying the innocence of perusing a pornographic magazine.

My mind went back to the big table with the butler lying on it and I turned to Ralph.

'Go down to the kitchen and see if those rolling pins are both there,' I said.

He went, glad to get out of the room, I think.

'Are you reducing this to farce?' said Alex. 'A rolling pin?'

'It is an excellent weapon for a smallish hand,' I said. 'And those hardwood ones in your kitchen would be most effective, even without a great deal of strength.'

'You suggest a woman killed him?'

Georgie and Alex spoke almost together, using nearly the same words.

'No, indeed not. I did not see a large pair of hands on anyone in this house. I always notice hands when it might have to do with serving food.'

'I see,' said Alex, unsatisfied.

'Of course, there are more women than men,' I said, going to the windows and looking behind the long curtains.

Charlie came up behind me.

'Found it?'

'No.'

'What do you think any crackpot did it for?'

I should have said, 'For part of the upstairs collection of horrors,' but didn't.

'There must have been a very good reason. It was feared that something would be found out.'

'And Dudley knew what.'

'Would it be about Clarence?' said Georgie.

There was no weapon behind the curtains. I turned round.

'Tell me about Clarence,' I said. 'Did he come here?'

'I wouldn't have mistaken him for someone else,' said Georgie, ironically.

'Why ask such a weird question?' Alex said.

Ralph came in.

'One has gone.' he said. 'Seems a pretty daft idea to try it out on the butler first. Suppose we'd found out who did that?'

'But we didn't,' said Alex, 'so he did this.'

'Why did he thump the butler, anyway?' said Ralph, looking round.

The family got more abstruse, as far as I was concerned.

Here was their brother, lying dead, brutally murdered, and they were intently talking about who biffed the butler. There was no sign of upset, sorrow, remorse; just an intense interest into the mental ways of the nut who'd done these things, thinking he could get away with it.

'It need not have been the same person,' I said. 'When one sees a way of doing things demonstrated it often happens one realises that it is a way of doing something one wishes could be done.'

'Yes, one one one does, don't one?' said Charlie, sarcastically.

'Could you say if anything was missing from here?' I said, hopefully.

'He put value on Nothing things,' said Georgie. 'Like pictures, books — not valuable ones, just ones he thought were beautiful.'

'Poor Dudley,' said Alex. 'I wish Fanny would come and shut his eyes. I can't look in that direction.'

'Your mother should be told, I think,' I said drily.

'Oh she won't come,' said Alex shortly. 'Death makes her vomit.' She wagged a hand at Ralph. 'Cover his face, for heaven's sake!'

Ralph looked round and finally covered the head with a jersey.

'The last time Clarence was seen here, according to what I've heard,' I said, 'he had his hat on because he'd been hit on the head.'

'The Phantom Head Basher strikes again,' said Georgie. 'But Clarence wasn't killed by his wallop, nor was the butler.'

'Must be coincidence,' said Ralph. 'Nobody would go round thumping like that. I still think the butler fell backwards. Anyhow, Alex said Clarence was hit in front.'

'Did she?' I said. In fact, Annie had

told me down at the pub. Alex hadn't seen because Clarence had had his hat on to cover it. So the story went.

'Well, he's been murdered,' said Charlie. 'The usual procedure is to call the police.'

'You'd have to have Mama's dead body for them to get in over,' said Georgie.

I felt a measure of relief and a great overmeasure of depression in the thought that, sooner or later, the police would come in, no matter what Mama said.

Ralph's idea in calling me was really to avoid calling the police in the first place. I should say, Ralph called me while thinking he was calling someone else.

'Leave the police out of it until Mr. Gaunt tells us what's best to do,' said Ralph.

And when he said that I realised that I was not so much in danger of being found out, as in extreme danger because I had been.

The story had been that Clarence had left the wish to have me called to find out his fate; that is, the man I was supposed to be whom Ralph had been told to call.

But had Ralph known from the beginning I wasn't Burlington? The first thing he had said was that he had expected me to look older, and then he had gone on with the rigmarole about the family and Clarence, and finally I had done more or less what he must have wanted.

I could not believe I had been a sucker to that extent, but now that I was watching the complete indifference in the family to a brother's murder, the odd thought struck me that they already had it in mind to slap it all on me.

That would relieve them of the worry of being found out and secure me against any careless talk about them in the future.

Future?

The word hurt me like being stabbed with an icicle.

I looked at their faces, calm, cunning, assured, evil, and felt I might have the same sort of future as Clarence had had.

'Well, Mr. Gaunt?' said Ralph.

'First,' I said, 'where is Clarence? Tell me or I'll have the police in and there'll be a quick end to all this acting the fool.'

'You all know what happened to him and where he is now. You all know who killed Dudley, so now is a good time to talk about it.'

'He's gone off his little nutty,' said Charlie, with a wondering look. 'Maybe somebody here knows what happened to Clarence, but I don't. I wish I did. He promised me something I didn't get.'

'Self, self, self,' said Alex, looking away. 'Clarence promised everybody. Shut up. What are we to do with this murder first? Somebody did it. That burglar you saw, Mr. Gaunt?'

'Why would a burglar be walking about with our rolling pin?' said Georgie contemptuously.

'That depends on who the burglar was,' said Alex calmly. 'If it's anyone who'd been in the kitchen already, he might have fancied taking one in case he wanted to roll someone out.'

'Stop being facetious!' Ralph shouted suddenly. 'It's our brother who's dead!'

'Is it?' said Georgie.

★ ★ ★

The significance of Georgie's remark put back the idea into my mind that Dudley had been arrived at from some other source than Van Deken.

But more important to me was the idea that I was not Burlington the investigator but his ex-partner from way back, so I was not so much a helping hand as a fall guy.

Not that I felt any conscience pricks if they did believe they'd got Burlington. He wasn't that good a detective. It had taken him five years to find me out, and that's a long time.

Anyhow, he was in South Africa for three months and far away from my conscience.

While I thought, I went on looking round the room, but untidiness made it difficult to see if anything had been disturbed.

Mama came in quite suddenly, with Fanny close behind.

'What's that?' said Mama, stopping. 'A body? Remove it at once! I won't have death in my house!'

She turned and swept out, quivering with dignity.

'You see?' said Alex, looking at me. 'She didn't even ask what's happened.'

The proper procedure for me was to ask where everybody had been, but they were all supposed to be in their bedrooms. Such questions were very likely to turn back on me.

I decided I should have to drop the jewels somewhere, as if the burglar had done the dropping in his haste.

But he hadn't been in haste, according to my story, until he had got outside and seen me.

He wouldn't have dropped anything before that, and I wasn't likely to get outside on my own.

I sat on the divan bed, looked at the body and then at the rest of the family.

'Let's talk,' I said. 'Ideas come that

way. Ralph, tell them what you did tonight.'

He shrugged.

'I asked Mr. Gaunt to come back,' he said. 'I let him in and asked him to take a look for Clarence up in the treasure room.'

'The front door was left unlocked,' I put in, as a form of self-defence.

'Well, did you go in that room?' said Charlie, staring.

'I did.'

'What did you find?' Georgie said very sharply.

'Stuff picked up from all over the world,' I said, 'including the rudimentary art of mummy making. There's a dead man up there, almost completely wound.'

'Who is it?' said Alex sharply.

'I don't know. Only the feet can be seen. I shouldn't think it's Clarence because of the time factor. I should think all that winding and stuff takes time.'

'Then who?' said Ralph, looking as if he didn't like the subject.

'Leave that. What did you expect me

to find up there? Clarence?'

'Oh no,' he said.

At the dining table the four had played an odd children's game where one was told of being hot or cold according to the rightness of the guess. The subject had been Clarence's body and each had said somewhere different, hoping another would deny it, but nobody had.

So it seemed that nobody had known. These children's attitudes of everything being a game, and nothing was real enough to be important, stretched even to the constant shrugging off the idea of getting the police in.

Unless they were a lot of crooks, but as they were rich anyway, and rarely left the house, it seemed absurd.

My notion that the riches might be fake had gone with the sight of Mama's heap of jewellery lying in amongst the hairpins, tweezers, hair combs and other rubbish. Anyone who could toss heaps like that about had lots of everything.

That didn't stop Clarence Marley from having some ready as well, but it cancelled my earlier theory.

In fact, I was cancelling all previous theories.

What I had to think of first was myself, as it seemed on the cards, as dealt by the Van Dekens, that I would be snared for burglary and a murder.

And further, brought there for the purpose of being slammed for these things.

Alex came and sat on the bed near me.

'Would it take practice to wind bandages round a body like that?' she said.

'It would take skill,' I said. 'First of all, you'd have to drain off all the blood and embalm the body and one needs to know all about it to do that. I don't, so I can't tell you any details of it.'

'Fanny would know,' said Georgie. 'About laying out the dead. She took a course.'

'Well, she'd only do that sort of thing for Mama,' said Alex.

'Or herself,' said Ralph.

It was the first time I had heard any of them defend Mama in any way at all.

186

'I don't think one person could do it,'
I said.

'Difficult, is it?' said Charlie.

'He said he didn't know,' said Georgie,
shortly.

'Who would know? It's about the
Babylonians or somebody. And why
would anybody want to keep a dead body
but some crackpot in primitive times?'

'I'm tired of this drivel,' said Alex,
looking at me rather oddly. 'I shall go
to bed with Mr. Gaunt.'

'I am flattered,' I said, taking her hand
as she offered it.

The others were watching. I got up.
So did Alex. She smiled at them
contemptuously.

We went together out of the room.
The others said nothing. We crossed the
corridor and went into a bedroom which
was lush; better than Mama's, and the
bed good enough for an empress. Two
Turners hung on the wall, themselves not
sixpenny pieces, and some of the smaller
ornaments, sold in the right markets,
could have kept me fastidiously for a
year or two.

She let go my hand as the door closed itself behind us, and turned her back to me as she faced the bed.

Whatever could be said of Mama and her daughters, lack of sexiness was not one of them. Clarence had not been able to help himself from involvement just as, I am afraid, Alex's suggestion to me had roused my mind vigorously.

As if she pulled a string which controlled all, she made a single movement and all she had on fell off and coiled round her feet in wreaths of silk. Then she turned to me smiling.

She was gorgeous. I felt I had to do what I intended at the start, for I would have been too easily persuaded against it later. I went and took her hands.

'First, tell me the truth,' I said.

'Oh no. It would spoil everything,' she said, and kissed me.

I kept her hands, with my fingers interlacing with hers. She put her head back as she tried to free her hands and I tightened my grip on them.

'You wouldn't — would you?' she said,

searching my eyes to find the answer. 'Hurt me?'

'Only until you told me.'

'You — ' She called me something I hadn't heard outside a barracks on fatigue day, then changed her mind and laughed. 'Go on then, savage. I won't tell you. I can't.'

# 10

I pushed her back on to the bed and held her there. She liked it and laughed.

'Rape me, then,' she said. 'I haven't had a rapist since Christmas.'

'You tempt me, then,' I said, 'but business first. You can tell me what you do know.'

'I am thinking of getting married again,' she said. 'You look my sort. Firm, resolute, dishonest — '

'How long was Clarence here before Mama shut herself up in her flat?'

'Oh, all of a day — maybe two — Come down beside me. I can't talk to you like that.'

I got on the bed beside her but held her hand firmly. It was a little difficult to keep my mind exactly on the complicated affair of Clarence.

Marrying had put my mind onto quite another road. Alex was a proposition on all counts, and even if she turned out to be a cow to live with she had plenty to make it bearable. Flesh and fleshpots, lust and lucre.

'Who do you think hit him that night?'

'I think he banged his head on something,' she said.

'I had an idea Fanny's room was supposed to be on the first floor, not the top.'

'She has one on both floors. The bottom one in case Mama is ill. Why keep on about Clarence? He is dead isn't he?'

I ran a finger down her neck.

'What difference would his death make to this family?'

'Materially? You know, if you do that, I shall rape *you*.' She grabbed my tie and pulled my head down and started kissing until I held her back a bit. 'Clarence?' she said, coming back to the question. 'None that I know of. Does it matter?'

'Apart from tonight, when did you last hear the water running in the attic?'

'You do scamper about in your little mind, don't you? When did it knock, you mean? Last night. Late. I thought Mama was having a bath.'

'Oh, you can hear it if anything runs?'

'Only Mama's. She's next along, you see.'

'Where did you get these cutaway dresses?'

'You'll make me dizzy, dodging from thing to thing like that.'

'Where? Tell me that and I won't ask any questions for a while.'

'Clarence. He got them made for a Christmas party when he was here last. Ten years back, now. And forget it. It was his idea of a joke — on the guests, of course. Now come here.'

I had thought of oysters, very thin brown bread and unsalted butter, cayenned and a slice of lemon with a few magical slivers of smoked salmon in pursuit; and then a pause for contemplation before the royal saddle of mutton — and then Annie. After that Charlie came into my fancy, and Georgie certainly, perhaps because of her pyjamas; but as I viewed the scene and the general aura of mature splendour, I was pleased without the oysters and salmon and mutton.

'You are kind,' I said.

'You are a sarcastic bastard,' she said. 'I'll marry you for what you are, and lord knows, that's pretty horrible. Come.'

The Van Deken family worked on tight schedule; each taking his cue on the instant.

No sooner had I decided to do without the oysters when somebody banged on the door.

'Come on out of that bed!' Charlie shouted through the panels. 'Mama's going to hang herself!'

Alex didn't get up but just shouted, 'Why?'

'She says she is a wicked woman and this is the best way for all of us,' said Charlie.

'I quite agree,' shouted Alex. 'Give her my best wishes for the future — if any.'

'Callous cow,' said Charlie. 'Fancy leaving it all to us!'

'Chuck a bucket of water over her!' shouted Alex. 'She won't hang herself if her hair looks a mess.'

I think it was then I started to laugh.

Alex sat up and laughed as well.

'I think we'd better go and see what the old bat's thinking about,' she said, picking her kimono off the bedrail. 'We'll resume the meeting later.'

'It'll be all right!' Georgie called, banging on the door at the same time. 'Ralph's gone in with the bucket.'

At almost the same time there was a fearful scream which sounded like another murder being done.

'It's all right. Ralph's emptied the bucket,' said Alex and started biting my ear. 'If we go into the burglary business together — the high class stuff only, of course — I should — '

'Flaming hell!' Charlie bawled. 'There's a mummy walking down the bloody stairs!'

'Let's get outside,' I said. 'Where's the key?'

She started looking round.

'What in hell did I do with it?' she said.

'You threw it somewhere on the bed! Quick!'

'Oh, don't panic,' she grumbled,

194

searching amongst the rumpled clothes. 'It's only a mummy.'

There was a wild shouting from outside in the passage and sounds as if they were all running away.

I knew in my heart that it must be my mummy coming down the stairs, so the man hadn't been dead at all, but his being alive and wrapped up like that presented a worse mystery than if he had been dead.

'Got it?' I said.

'Don't shout!' she said angrily and bent to look under the bed. 'Can't you pick the lock or something? I don't know where I dropped it.'

There was an almighty crash, some of the door frame split out and the mummy walked in.

'What kind of a detective are you?' the Mummy cried, rather muffled because he was speaking through a slit between the bandages round his face.

'A bad one,' I said.

'Get me out of this bloody outfit! The bloody zip's stuck!'

'You're a worse mummy than you are

a butler,' I said. 'Turn round. I can't find the zipper.'

'It's well hidden,' he grumbled. 'Its a stage prop. You can't go walking about the stage with a bloody great zip showing up your backside.'

'You speak Australian well,' I said. 'Hold on! I've got it.' I found the small white plastic tab and pulled. It came off in my hand. 'There now. It's broken and you're locked in.'

'What did you do it for?' Alex said. 'Dressing up like that!'

'It was a joke. It was going to be a good joke. But everybody kept getting in the way and the promised visit to the attic didn't come off. Only the eye came and it would have been wasted on him.'

'Who promised the visit?'

'Dudley was going to organise it. Something must have put him off.'

I got him by the shoulder, turned him then threw him face down across the bed and stucked my knee right in the middle of his back so that for him to move would have been very painful indeed.

He didn't say anything.

'What are you doing — ?' Alex began, coming towards us.

'Stay right back,' I said. 'He's strong. He bust the door in, remember.' The mummy stayed still under my knee.

'Who hit you on the head?' I said.

'A woman. I don't know which one. Only saw legs before I got it.'

'I thought you were paid to go away, with compensation,' I said.

'Yes,' he said, and then, 'yes and no, that is. I don't accept it as full liability.'

He had seen my trap, but too late. He knew I had been in the attic, and had lain dogo for the purpose of not being discovered by me.

It meant he had been up in the attic before Ralph had unlocked the house and let me in.

'So all this was a gag, designed to frighten the daylights out of the inmates?' I said, grinding my knee a bit into his back.

'Easy, easy!' he pleaded. 'I don't want to slip a disc.'

'Was it?'

'Yes.'

'Whose idea?'

'Clarence put me up to it.'

I saw Alex watching with acute attention.

'When did you see him?'

'Day before yesterday.'

'Where?'

'Down the pub. There's a pub backs on to the grounds here.'

'Did he have any other ideas for gags like that?'

'He wanted to shake 'em. He wanted to really shake 'em.'

'So what did he suggest apart from the mummy gag?'

'He was going to pretend he was dead so they'd all get shook to their bases.'

'But why should that shake them? Was it going to be a murder?'

'Of course. So they'd all suspect each other, and then when they was all stewed up, down I come as the walking dead etcetera.'

'So it was all to be a hoax?'

'Sure, sport. Sure.'

'Then he'd pay you?'

'You bet he would.'

'Where were you to meet him?'

'Same place. The pub.'

'When?'

'Tomorrow.'

'Is he telling the truth?' Alex said, looking at me very hard.

'Partly, because part of it fits.'

I took my knee off his back and went and stood by Alex.

The reason I did so was because Ralph walked in with a double barrel shotgun at the ready, and by then I knew enough about Ralph to make me cautious.

Not knowing what had happened behind him, the mummy got up from the bed and turned in the direction of the door.

Ralph fired the gun, and the mummy bent over as if kicked in the stomach, then collapsed to the floor.

★ ★ ★

Though the room was very large and there must have been plenty of room for absorption of the noise, it sounded like a small bomb.

'What on earth did you do that for?' shouted Alex. 'We were talking to him! He was giving us the griff!'

Ralph wiped his face with an open hand and looked as if he were not sure of what he had done.

It was a difficult moment, standing at the end of the bed with Ralph twenty feet away holding the gun with one barrel still charged.

The noise brought the others out, fears of walking dead overcame by curiosity about who'd been shot.

Of the family, Mama was last, and for whom, as usual, the offspring made a path so she could see and walk into the room if she wanted to.

She came up behind Ralph.

'What have you done this time, you bloody great fool?' she said, looking at Ralph, but not at the mummy. 'Put that instrument down at once!'

Slowly, he broke it and then held it

under his arm, with the one chamber still loaded.

'Now, Mr. Gaunt, what have *you* done now?' said Mama, coming right into the room.

Georgie and Charlie both came in, but Fanny was not there.

When I saw them all gathering like that, I began to realise what sort of a trap I had run into.

As an investigator, I was out of practice or I should have seen it earlier than I did.

At the start they had come to me one after the other, each with a different story in several senses, yet each with the same thing in common.

Clarence had been murdered. They had all said that.

The excuses about not getting the police had suited me very well, for from the start, it had been in my mind to take a sample of the renowned possessions of the Van Deken family. And I had carried that out.

Greed, careful planning, art and skill had gone into the gaining of a profit in my pocket; but they seemed to have understood my weakness from the beginning.

Letting me in at night, leaving Mama's door open with a good deal of noise calling attention to its openness was very obvious a ploy when one saw it afterwards.

One tends to be blinded by the need to possess at certain times.

I had got what I had meant to get, but now I had it, I was like the monkey and the jar where he grabs a fistful of nuts and can't get his fist out of the neck of the jar.

I had had a busy evening, an entertaining evening up to a point: a frightening, nightmarish evening in the attic, and now a dead loss of an evening in Alex's bedroom with the clan gathered around me.

And I had nothing against them as far as Clarence was concerned. I had found nothing at all to show that he was dead.

I had nothing to pin on these people but Dudley's death and I had found nothing about that but the body.

'Who's in the gift wrapper?' said Charlie, nodding at the mummy.

And that was the final blow to me; for I had seen that killing, which would certainly be put up as a defence act.

Except that Ralph knew who it was.

My spirits rose. Ralph had said he had paid off the butler and sent him out of the house, but the butler had never gone.

Ralph, therefore, knew about this mummy gag.

When Dudley had been walloped, Alex, Mama and Fanny had been out of sight, and the butler might have come down to the first floor before he had been seen to do so.

I was sure Dudley had been swiped because he was the only one who had been genuinely worried about the whole business of Clarence's disappearance.

The others had been playing their game, caring only about Clarence's fate inasmuch as they thought it might affect their immediate comfort.

It seemed that the killing of Clarence, if

it had taken place, had been a community effort, or at the very least, they all knew when, where and how it had happened.

And then there had been the game at the dinner table; making up lies of knowing where the body was, in the hope that the one who did know would give it away.

All right. Clarence was murdered as a club effort, but afterwards, one person had taken and hidden the body, and the others were desperately anxious to know where it was so that there was no danger of the public suddenly finding it and bringing the law on the Van Dekens.

That must be the answer to the whole rigmarole. Not calling me to find a murder, but to find the body to protect the murderers.

And I had been so suitable for this purpose, with my weakness liable to break out any moment in a place so full of beautiful things, all worth money one way or another.

The reason why everyone had said they did not know where the body was had been the truth, not a herring trailer.

So, as far as they were concerned, they would have a body finder and a safety lock on him at the same time, so what had seemed incongruous at first now looked highly intelligent.

And further, I had a thousand-pound cheque which would certainly be offered as proof, if ever necessary, that I had been paid for silence over Clarence and his end.

Who could believe in that sum being paid for a normal service? Some people, perhaps, but no police-man.

Once more I regarded the faces watching me, and I realised that it would be a touch and go business as to whether I ever got out of the place except in a coffin or garbage crate.

'What happened to Fanny?' I said. 'There should have been enough noise to wake her and bring her down here.'

'Fetch her, Charlie!' said Mama. 'She's using the room down here, not upstairs. I thought she was up there myself, for the night that is, but no, full of whim, she shifted down here without a word to anyone.

'She isn't here,' I said.

'How do you know?' said Mama.

'It's a guess. But while standing here fearing the worst, my mind saw a light in the fog.'

'What light?' said Alex.

'Sex,' I said. 'Clarence suffered a surfeit of it and amongst the entertainers may be one who is not quite sophisticated enough and got jealous. Jealousy is very simple, but very powerful.'

'Well?' said Mama.

'Such murders are always spur-of-the-moment affairs and can happen in crowded places.'

'We know all about that,' said Mama impatiently.

'I know you do.'

'Where is he now?' said Georgie.

Charlie came back.

'She has gone. Packed,' she said. 'I suppose she got the wind up.'

'*Now* what am I going to do about my hair?' said Mama, angrily.

'She hopped it because she brained Dudley,' said Georgie. 'One of the family wouldn't do it. Besides, we could be sure

Dudley didn't talk outside, but Fanny couldn't. After all this time she didn't know about the Van Deken Mafia. How dumb!'

'Some people just look at themselves,' said Alex, piously. 'No thought for others unless they get paid for it.'

'I paid her!' cried Mama.

The argument went on while I mentally reproved myself for having looked at myself all the time and having let my mind frighten me.

Why, a sink in an attic might have been used solely for washing hands after touching dusty goods. Paints, pots, brushes for repairs.

'It's all been rather a mess,' said Alex to me. 'It was a terrible mix-up and Dudley shouting 'incest' and lord knows what, although Clarence was only half everything to us, and he got biffed on the head with a rolling pin, so he went out to the pub after telling us he'd wipe us all up when he got back.'

And it could all really have been so innocent of sin; nothing more than the errors of righteous impetuosity. Murders are often like that. If I found it paid.

I realised I was less worried than they were about it and if it all paid me at the end, instead of resulting in my demise, then it would all have been worth while.

'I won't rest until I know where they hid Clarence, whoever did that hiding!' said Mama. 'He was killed accidentally by everybody — well, it was unfortunate Ralph had the gun — that bloody gun, Ralph! Why did you get it out again?'

Ralph didn't answer, I didn't interfere. He still had a loaded barrel and snapping the gun back into position was the work of a split second.

Ralph had been attentive to Mary. Ralph had driven Mary home when she had been thrown out. Ralph had been jealous over Mary.

The accident in the rough and tumble had been more than likely, with Ralph meaning to do it.

I felt relieved that at least I knew who'd done it after all. Ralph knew he was taking no risks calling me, anyhow. Clarence had told him my reputation for certain, because the reason why Clarence had said to call my ex-partner was that they knew each other.

How else would he have had such an inspiration? When he thought he would be topped? He had mentioned Burlington, and gone on to say how his partner had been a dedicated jewel thief, for long undiscovered, as an amusing aside.

But the dedicated jewel thief, apparent detective, was just what Ralph wanted when somebody stole the body, and he had acted fast.

I couldn't understand, however, how by a phone call he had known I had answered and not Burlington.

And there was the answer, lying flat on the mat. The butler.

With rather a foolish overestimation of my own value in the past, I had not thought that Burlington might have taken on a rough partner for collecting debts and so forth, and that partner also an acquaintance of Clarence who would do anything for a pound or two, such as tip Ralph when I came in the office with the key I never gave up.

And now, to save all this complicated business coming out, Ralph had pooped him off.

As, I suppose I smiled with pleasure at my solution to at least the beginning of the problem.

When I looked up, Ralph put the gun together again, watching me the while, and I felt a sudden chill, because there was nowhere for me to escape.

I was about to receive what I had deserved by not being sharp enough and the family and Mama stood back to give him plenty of elbow room.

He raised the gun to his sight. It was an unforgettable moment.

Then two things happened at once.

Alex grabbed my arm and pulled me to her side.

'Don't you dare! I'm going to marry him!'

The women started saying, 'What? *What?* Whaaat!'

Which almost covered the first groan which emanated from the mummy on the floor. The doubling of bandages and the lining underneath them had been thick enough to spread the shot.

'Let's go to my place,' I said to Alex.

'Of course,' she said, and let my arm go to fetch a fur coat from the dressing table chair.

Ralph stood as if unsure what to do at all.

Alex slipped on the coat and came back to me. We walked to the door. For a change, the family parted for us instead of, as usual, just for Mama.

At the door I stopped Alex and looked back.

'Sex, I said, if you remember. Mostly in bedrooms. If you want to find the unfortunate Clarence I suggest you look in Mary's bedroom — the one nobody's been in since she left. Fanny is such a big, strong woman, you know. Goodnight.'

## Other titles in the
## Linford Mystery Library

### A LANCE FOR THE DEVIL
#### Robert Charles

The funeral service of Pope Paul VI was to be held in the great plaza before St. Peter's Cathedral in Rome, and was to be the scene of the most monstrous mass assassination of political leaders the world had ever known. Only Counter-Terror could prevent it.

### IN THAT RICH EARTH
#### Alan Sewart

How long does it take for a human body to decay until only the bones remain? When Detective Sergeant Harry Chamberlane received news of a body, he raised exactly that question. But whose was the body? Who was to blame for the death and in what circumstances?

## MURDER AS USUAL
### Hugh Pentecost

A psychotic girl shot and killed Mac Crenshaw, who had come to the New England town with the advance party for Senator Farraday. Private detective David Cotter agreed that the girl was probably just a pawn in a complex game — but who had sent her on the assignment?

## THE MARGIN
### Ian Stuart

It is rumoured that Walkers Brewery has been selling arms to the South African army, and Graham Lorimer is asked to investigate. He meets the beautiful Shelley van Rynveld, who is dedicated to ending apartheid. When a Walkers employee is killed in a hit-and-run accident, his wife tells Graham that he's been seeing Shelly van Rynveld . . .

## TOO LATE FOR THE FUNERAL
### Roger Ormerod
Carol Turner, seventeen, and a mystery, is very close to a murder, and she has in her possession a weapon that could prove a number of things. But it is Elsa Mallin who suffers most before the truth of Carol Turner releases her.

## NIGHT OF THE FAIR
### Jay Baker
The gun was the last of the things for which Harry Judd had fought and now it was in the hands of his worst enemy, aimed at the boy he had tried to help. This was the night in which the past had to be faced again and finally understood.

## MR CRUMBLESTONE'S EDEN
Henry Crumblestone was a quiet little man who would never knowingly have harmed another, and it was a dreadful twist of irony that caused him to kill in defence of a dream . . .

## PAY-OFF IN SWITZERLAND
### Bill Knox

'Hot' British currency was being smuggled to Switzerland to be laundered, hidden in a safari-style convoy heading across Europe. Jonathan Gaunt, external auditor for the Queen's and Lord Treasurer's Remembrancer, went along with the safari, posing as a tourist, to get any lead he could. But sudden death trailed the convoy every kilometer to Lake Geneva.


## SALVAGE JOB
### Bill Knox

A storm has left the oil tanker S.S. *Craig Michael* stranded and almost blocking the only channel to the bay at Cabo Esco. Sent to investigate, marine insurance inspector Laird discovers that the Portuguese bay is hiding a powder keg of international proportions.

## BOMB SCARE — FLIGHT 147
### Peter Chambers

Smog delayed Flight 147, and so prevented a bomb exploding in mid-air. Walter Keane found that during the crisis he had been robbed of his jewel bag, and Mark Preston was hired to locate it without involving the police. When a murder was committed, Preston knew the stake had grown.

## STAMBOUL INTRIGUE
### Robert Charles

Greece and Turkey were on the brink of war, and the conflict could spell the beginning of the end for the Western defence pact of N.A.T.O. When the rumour of a plot to speed this possibility reached Counter-espionage in Whitehall, Simon Larren and Adrian Cleyton were despatched to Turkey . . .

## CRACK IN THE SIDEWALK
### Basil Copper

After brilliant scientist Professor Hopcroft is knocked down and killed by a car, L.A. private investigator Mike Faraday discovers that his death was murder and that differing groups are engaged in a power struggle for The Zetland Method. As Mike tries to discover what The Zetland Method is, corpses and hair-breadth escapes come thick and fast . . .


## DEATH OF A MACHINE
### Charles Leader

When Mike M'Call found the mutilated corpse of a marine in an alleyway in Singapore, a thousand-strong marine battalion was hell-bent on revenge for their murdered comrade — and the next target for the tong gang of paid killers appeared to be M'Call himself . . .

## ANYONE CAN MURDER
### Freda Bream

Hubert Carson, the editorial Manager of the Herald Newspaper in Auckland, is found dead in his office. Carson's fellow employees knew that the unpopular chief reporter, Clive Yarwood, wanted Carson's job — but did he want it badly enough to kill for it?

## CART BEFORE THE HEARSE
### Roger Ormerod

Sometimes a case comes up backwards. When Ernest Connelly said 'I have killed . . . ', he did not name the victim. So Dave Mallin and George Coe find themselves attempting to discover a body to fit the crime.

## SALESMAN OF DEATH
### Charles Leader

For Mike M'Call, selling guns in Detroit proves a dangerous business — from the moment of his arrival in the middle of a racial plot, to the final clash of arms between two rival groups of militant extremists.

418